How to Survive Your First Bridge Tournament

How to Survive Your First Bridge Tournament

DAVID BURN

faber and faber
LONDON · BOSTON

First published in 1993
by Faber and Faber Limited
3 Queen Square London WC1N 3AU

Photoset by Parker Typesetting Service, Leicester
Printed in England by Clays Ltd, St Ives plc

David Burn is hereby identified as author of this work in
accordance with Section 77 of the Copyright, Designs and
Patents Act 1988

A CIP record for this book is available from the British Library

ISBN 0–571–16499–4

2 4 6 8 10 9 7 5 3 1

Contents

Introduction

This, as the title implies, is a book primarily for players who are wondering whether to move from bridge at the local club to the wider tournament field. Many people find their first bridge tournament a daunting experience, for they encounter a more strictly controlled and more serious atmosphere than they find at the friendly local duplicate. There are strange pieces of paper to be filled in, officials giving all manner of instructions, opponents who play all kinds of strange conventions. There are additional rules to be followed in tournament play which may not all be observed in every bridge club. Often, players find all this difficult to handle, and are not able to do themselves justice in terms of bridge skill because the atmosphere and the mechanics of the tournament game are overwhelming.

Do not worry. It is many years now since I played my first tournament, but I assure you that I was every bit as nervous as you are. Even though I have played thousands of tournaments since then, I am still excited and apprehensive at the challenge that each new competition presents. I hope that this book will encourage you to enter the world of tournament bridge, and that you may take from it some points which will enable you to give of your best from your very first tournament onwards.

This book is not solely for newcomers, though. The main part of the book is a narrative which follows a young pair through just part of their first major pairs tournament. Each triumph and each disaster is discussed, and the technical points which arise may help even the experienced player to do a little better in the next tournament he or she enters. The first section deals with the mechanics of tournament bridge, so if you are already familiar with those, you can skip to the second section and start reading about the bridge itself.

This is not a textbook. It does not attempt to teach specific aspects of the game in any kind of detail. After every hand, there is a discussion of the points which arose in the bidding and the play, but this discussion is designed to give you no more than a few ideas on what constitutes good play at the pairs game. Take what seems of value to you and discard the rest – there are innumerable systems and conventions in the tournament world these days, and it is not my intention to recommend to you any but the most basic treatments in either bidding or play. Should you feel the need to investigate any of the ideas in this book in more detail, the companion books to this one in Faber and Faber's new list will provide you with all the information you could desire.

One of the beauties of tournament bridge is that at no other sport is it possible for a newcomer to enter a competition and play against the very best in the game. Of course, this can be daunting – you will probably be outclassed and come off second best. But every once in a while, you will experience the real thrill of beating the experts, sometimes through good fortune, but often through your own skill. My hope in writing this book is that one day, you and I may meet at the bridge table and that you will use the advice in these pages to beat me at my own game.

The Tournament Begins

Pat and Chris peered nervously at the notice boards outside the ballroom of the seaside hotel which was the venue for their first ever national bridge tournament. An array of lists indicated where all the players were supposed to sit for the qualifying round of the Pairs Championship, the major event of the weekend. Pat was the first to spot their names, North–South at table seven in what was cryptically described as the Green Section. She looked around anxiously for someone to tell her where the Green Section was, and how it was to be distinguished from all the others – red, purple, black and most of the rest of the colours of the spectrum. A man in a bow tie and evening dress noticed her predicament.

'Can I help you, madam?' he enquired politely.

'Not just now, thanks,' said Pat, taking him for a waiter. 'I'm trying to find someone to tell me about this tournament.'

'I am the Chief Tournament Director,' said that official urbanely, 'and I would be happy to answer any questions you may have.'

'Oh', said Pat. 'Well, where is table seven in the Green Section, please?'

'The Green Section is in the far corner of the ballroom,' said the Director. 'It has green table number cards, and table seven is the one with a number seven on it. The North seat is the one facing the stage.'

'Thank you,' said Pat. 'Come on, Chris, we'd better find our table.'

In tournaments involving a very large number of pairs, the field is divided into sections of around thirteen tables. Each section is treated as separate for the purposes of the movement – if you are an East–West pair, then at the end of each round you move to the next higher numbered table in your section. The same boards are played in all the sections, though, and the scoring is done 'across the field' – that is, your score on any deal is compared with those of all the other pairs in the event sitting the same way as you are.

When Pat and Chris had found their table, they discovered various pieces of stationery on it. One was a name slip, whose purpose baffled Chris. 'Obviously,' he said, 'they must know that we are North–South at table seven in the Green Section, so why do we have to fill out a name slip?'

'It's just a check,' said the gentleman who was sitting in the East seat. 'Sometimes people don't turn up, and sometimes the Directors have to move pairs around to make the movement easier, so although in theory they know who you are, it helps if you tell them again.'

'Right,' said Chris. 'You seem to know your way around – could you tell me what this envelope is for?'

'You address that to yourselves,' said East, 'and then they can send you the results of the tournament plus any Master Points you may win. You have to fill out a certificate for those – here it is.'

Pat and Chris looked at a couple of postcard-sized objects which bore the legend: Master Point Certificate. They knew what Master Points were – in club events and tournament events, success is rewarded by Master Points which, when accumulated, allow players to move up the English Bridge Union's ranking ladder. This starts at the bottom with Club Master – 200 Master Points – and extends to the exalted rank of Grand Master, which requires millions of the things, including points in a special category available only in National tournaments.

Chris addressed the envelope, then he and Pat filled in their names on the Master Point Certificates. Just as they had finished this, the Chief Tournament Director mounted the stage at the end of the ballroom and spoke into a microphone.

'Ladies and gentlemen,' he said, 'please would you complete the name slips on your table, and fill in the Master Point cards. There are two envelopes on your table – one for each partnership, which you should address to yourselves. When you have finished that, you can save a little time by putting the cards in each board into suits, ready for duplication.'

Pat reached for the two duplicate boards on the table – plastic wallets with compartments marked North, South, East and West. These are used to enable the same deals to be played at all tables in a tournament. At the start of a deal, you take your cards out of the slot in the wallet which corresponds to your compass position. Cards are not played during the hand by throwing them into the centre of the table and gathering up tricks. Instead, each player puts his card face up in front of him. When the trick is over, the cards are turned face down. The side which wins the trick turns their cards over so that the shorter edge is parallel to their edge of the table. The side which loses the trick turns their cards so that the longer edge runs parallel to their edge of the table. At the end of the deal, each player has the same thirteen cards with which he started face down in a row, turned so that it is possible to count the number of tricks won and lost. The cards are then picked up and returned to the wallet, ready for play at the next table. Sometimes, rigid plastic or wooden boards are used instead of wallets, and it is common to refer to each deal as a 'board'. The boards are numbered in sequence, and the dealer and vulnerability are indicated on each board.

In tournaments with a number of sections, the players 'duplicate' the boards on their table prior to the first playing round. The hands are dealt by a computer, which prints out little slips called 'curtain cards' on which the hands are recorded. At the start of each hand, it is a rule that you must take your cards out of the board and count them face down before looking at them.

When you are satisfied that you have thirteen cards, you look at your hand and the accompanying curtain card to check that they match. In this way, it is possible for errors to be corrected – should some cards have been mixed up at the preceding table, or should some clowns have replaced their hands in the wrong pockets of the board, this can be detected before play begins at the next table.

Pat was just about to take the cards out of one of the two boards on her table when West stopped her. 'It's all right,' he said. 'We've already suited the boards.' This meant that East and West had arranged the packs into suits, to simplify the next task which the table would undertake.

'The Tournament Directors are giving out the curtain cards now,' said the Chief Tournament Director. 'When you receive them, please make up the boards. Then, mark the travelling score slips with the board number and section colour and put them in the boards.'

As he spoke, another evening-suited figure approached their table and deposited two cardboard strips in front of Chris, who was South. He picked them up and saw that they were perforated, and that each strip contained four curtain cards for the two boards that were on their table. Hoping to look as though he had been doing this all his life, he tore the strips into four and gave the two North hands to Pat, the East hands to the gentleman on his left and the West hands to the player on his right.

East looked at the two pieces of cardboard, then solemnly handed them to West and received the East curtain cards from his partner in exchange. Chris blushed deeply, and West took pity on him. 'We're quite happy to do the duplication,' he said, 'but be ready to check it afterwards, won't you?'

So saying, he collected one set of curtain cards while East picked up the other. Picking up one of the suited packs of cards, he dealt them into four piles at bewildering speed, put one

4

curtain card on top of each pile, placed the hands in the board and looked up triumphantly at East.

'Far too slow,' said that individual, who had already finished duplicating his board and had summoned a passing waiter. 'Two coffees, please,' he said, and indicated his partner. 'This gentleman will pay.'

'Not if you've made a mistake,' said West. 'Check the boards for us, please,' he added to Pat and Chris.

Each picked up a board and compared the hands in turn with the corresponding curtain cards. There were no errors, and Pat almost burst into applause, for the whole thing had been done with the speed and confidence of a conjuring trick. 'Fifteen years,' said West resignedly, 'and I haven't managed to get a coffee out of him yet. The meanness of some people is beyond belief.'

East had picked up his pen and was writing the board numbers and the word 'Green' on the travelling score slips, which he placed in the appropriate boards. A travelling score slip, as its name implies, 'travels' with each board in its progress from table to table. As each deal is played, it is the responsibility of the North player to fill in, on the topmost free line of the slip, the North–South and East–West pair numbers, the contract, the number of tricks made and the score to North–South or East–West.

Each deal is a separate entity at duplicate, unlike at rubber bridge where contracts which are made count towards game and rubber. A bonus of 50 is awarded for making a part score contract, so three hearts bid and made scores 140 (90 plus 50). If overtricks are made, they are simply added to the total score – there is no such thing as 'above' or 'below the line' at duplicate, so two no trumps making four scores 180 (130 plus 50). A bonus of 300 is given for a non-vulnerable game (remember, the vulnerability is indicated on the board), and 500 for a vulnerable game. Slam bonuses are the same as at rubber bridge and are awarded in addition to the game bonus, so a non-vulnerable six diamonds bid and made scores 920 (120 plus 300 for game plus 500 for a non-vulnerable small slam). The slam bonuses are:

	Non-Vulnerable	Vulnerable
Small	500	750
Grand	1000	1500

Undertricks are scored as at rubber bridge under the new Laws – in fact, the additional penalties for non-vulnerable doubled undertricks were introduced at duplicate before coming into force at rubber bridge. They are:

	Non-vulnerable	Vulnerable
Undoubled	50	100
Doubled	1st 100	1st 200
	2nd and 3rd 200	Others 300
	Others 300	
Redoubled	1st 200	1st 400
	2nd and 3rd 400	Others 600
	Others 600	

The bonus for making a double contract is 50 points, for a redoubled contract 100 points.

The objective at pairs scoring, again unlike rubber bridge, is not to outscore your opponents at the table – they may hold better cards than you do. Rather, you are trying to outscore the other pairs sitting in the same direction as you who hold the same cards as you do. For each pair that you outscore, you are given two match points. For each pair whose score is the same as yours, you are given one match point, and for each pair who outscores you, you receive no match points. For example, when a board has been played at six tables, the travelling score slip may look something like this:

Board number 12

NS	EW	Contract	By	Tricks	Score		MPs	
					NS	EW	NS	EW
1	1	4 ♠	N	11	650		7	5
2	3	3 NT	N	10	630		4	8
3	5	6 ♠	N	11		100	0	10
4	7	4 ♠	N	11	650		7	5
5	6	4 ♠	N	10	620		2	8
6	4	3 NT	N	11	660		10	0

It will be seen that the North–South pair who played in 3NT with two overtricks have the best, or 'top' North–South score. The pair who played in 6 ♠ going down have the worst, or 'bottom', score. One frequently hears players discussing their scores in terms of 'tops' and 'bottoms'.

This form of scoring means that the tactics used for success at pairs are on occasion very different from those used at rubber bridge. We will see as the tournament develops some of the considerations that this special form of scoring requires as far as your play is concerned. Not all of them, by any means – whole books can be and have been written on special tactics for match-pointed pairs, and this is not one of them – but it is vitally important that you understand the implications of this form of scoring. The most important is this: *you must never give up fighting for tricks.* If you can see that you have ten easy tricks in four spades, then at rubber bridge you might be inclined to take your eye of the ball and overlook a play that would give you a chance of eleven – 'it's only an overtrick,' after all. At pairs, as you can perhaps see from the travelling score slip above, such lapses of concentration can have a serious effect on your overall score.

Pairs tournaments are run in one of two main ways. Either the whole field is involved throughout the tournament – which may be one session of play or as many as four or five – or there is a qualifying round and a final (possibly a semi-final if the tournament is very large). The tournament in which Chris and Pat are about to play is run on the second principle, and they are about to play the qualifying session of twenty-four boards. If they finish in the top third of the field, then they will progress to the next round; if not, there will be a 'Consolation' event running at the same time as the semi-final stage.

Deal 1

'When you have checked the duplication,' came the Chief Director's voice from the microphone, 'will the East–West pairs move to the next higher numbered table, and will the North players move the boards to the next lower numbered table. Then please start play for the first round.'

'Good luck!' said East and West as they left the table.

'Same to you,' said Chris, reaching behind him to collect the boards that were being passed from the next table.

The two young men who replaced the departing East–West pair were casually but smartly dressed, and greeted Pat and Chris with exemplary politeness. They each handed over a convention card which announced that they were playing a basically natural system, but on which every bid from the two level upwards appeared to have any one of a number of possible meanings.

Pat and Chris exchanged their own very much simpler convention card with the opponents, each of whom studied it briefly but keenly. It looked, thought Chris as he removed his cards from the board for the first hand of his first tournament, as though they had not been afforded the easiest pair of opponents against whom to start.

Chris was relieved to find that he held a good hand and was the dealer – he had been dreading the opponents' opening the bidding with one of their conventional gadgets and having to cope. These were his cards:

♠ A K 10 5 2
♡ 6
♢ K Q J 7
♣ K Q 6

He opened proceedings with the obvious one spade. West passed and Pat responded with a jump to three spades. What action would you take now on Chris's hand?

This is not an easy decision, for although the raise to three spades has a fairly narrow range in Acol – about 9–11 points, or eight losers if the Losing Trick Count system of valuation is employed – there is a very wide range of 9–11 point hands that partner can hold. This hand, for example:

♠ Q 7 6 3
♡ A 9 8 4
♢ 6 2
♣ A 10 9

would give Chris an almost certain play for six spades, while this:

♠ 7 6 4 3
♡ K Q 9 3
♢ 4
♣ A J 10 7

would certainly not make anything above game, and might not even make that if the breaks were bad.

Chris was usually the steadier player of the partnership – a sound, dependable bidder who was content to leave aggression and flights of imagination to Pat. In mitigation of what he did next, it should be pointed out that these were abnormal circumstances. He was keyed up, desperately anxious to start the tournament well, and a little nervous of his young opponents. Altogether, he was not quite in full possession of his faculties when, in ringing tones, he declaimed: 'Four no-trumps!'

Pat tapped the table, indicating a conventional call, and West smiled at her. 'Quite right,' he said. 'Doesn't sound natural, does it?'

West passed, and Pat bid five diamonds. That was a blow to Chris, who had been hoping for a response of five hearts so that he could soar into a slam and trust to his guardian angel to look after the trump suit if necessary. Still, there were two aces missing, so he settled for five spades.

'Double,' said West quietly.

The effect on Pat and Chris was electrifying. Pat dropped three of her cards on the floor, where they landed face downwards. Chris turned various shades of crimson as he realized to his horror the implications of the double – not only were there two missing aces, but West presumably had at least one and perhaps two tricks in trumps. East, beyond shifting his chair back from the table so that Pat could more easily pick up her cards, was totally unperturbed.

The auction ended with three passes, and West detached a card from his hand which he placed face downwards on the table.

'Four no-trumps?' enquired East of Pat.

'Blackwood,' she said, puzzled. What else could it be, after all?

'Just simple Blackwood? Not Roman or anything?' persisted East.

'No,' said Pat, wondering what her opponent was talking about. 'Just asking for aces.'

'Thank you,' said East politely, and West turned over his opening lead, which was the four of hearts. Pat spread her dummy, and Chris saw that his worst fears were realized. The full deal was:

North–South Vulnerable.
Dealer South.

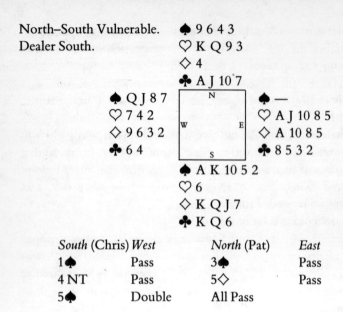

♠ 9 6 4 3
♡ K Q 9 3
♢ 4
♣ A J 10 7

♠ Q J 8 7
♡ 7 4 2
♢ 9 6 3 2
♣ 6 4

♠ —
♡ A J 10 8 5
♢ A 10 8 5
♣ 8 5 3 2

♠ A K 10 5 2
♡ 6
♢ K Q J 7
♣ K Q 6

South (Chris)	West	North (Pat)	East
1♠	Pass	3♠	Pass
4 NT	Pass	5♢	Pass
5♠	Double	All Pass	

East won dummy's king of hearts with the ace and cashed the ace of diamonds. When, as Chris had feared, East showed out on the first round of spades, Chris simply conceded two trump tricks to West without further ado.

'Two down,' he mumbled. 'Sorry, Pat.'

'Smart double,' said East to his partner. West smiled deprecatingly. 'It was unlucky for them,' he said. 'But I think that if . . .'

His words tailed off in confusion, for he was a polite young man and had no wish to add to the already considerable misery of his opponents by pointing out that Chris could have saved a trick. Try to work out what line of play West had in mind.

Post Mortem

Chris's jump to Blackwood was not totally ridiculous, but it was over-ambitious. It is true that Pat might have had exactly the right cards to make a slam cold – two aces and the ♠Q – but in general it is expecting too much to play partner for three specific 'right cards' on this type of auction. Besides, there was another option available.

Four level slam tries
It happens frequently that your side locates a fit at the three level, and that one hand (or both) has reserves of strength. While Blackwood can be the right answer in certain circumstances, it is usually better to proceed by means of cue-bids or trial bids at the four level. It is important to agree a number of points with your partner in this type of auction.

What would you bid with this hand:

> ♠ A K 10 5 2
> ♡ 6
> ♢ A Q 9 7 5
> ♣ A 2

after opening one spade and being raised to three spades?

The success or failure of a slam contract is almost certain to depend on whether partner can provide help in the diamond suit. Facing:

> ♠ Q 9 7 3
> ♡ A 7 4
> ♢ K J 3
> ♣ 7 5

there is an excellent play for seven spades, but if partner has:

> ♠ 7 6 4 3
> ♡ K Q J 4
> ♢ 8 6 2
> ♣ K Q

You have no desire at all to be any higher than four spades, and you might not even make that on a really bad day.

A number of expert pairs play that after one of a major has been raised to three, a new suit at the four level is a 'trial bid' – that is, a suit in which help in the form of a high honour is required for slam. This is similar to the bid of a new suit as a game try after one of a major has been raised to two, which we will discuss later. On our example hands, the auctions might be:

♠ A K 10 5 2	♠ Q 9 7 3	1♠	3♠
♡ 6	♡ A 7 4 2	4◇[1]	4♡[2]
◇ A Q 9 7 5	◇ K J 3	5♣[3]	5◇[4]
♣ A 2	♣ 7 5	5 NT[5]	6◇[6]
		7♠	Pass

[1] Long suit slam try.
[2] Cue-bid, accepting the try because of the diamond fit.
[3] Cue-bid – first-round control. Note that 4◇ has not denied the ♣A.
[4] Cue-bid, showing the fitting diamond honour.
[5] Asking for top spade honours.
[6] One of the ♠A, ♠K or ♠Q.

♠ A K 10 5 2	♠ 7 6 4 3	1♠	3♠
♡ 6	♡ K Q J 4	4◇	4♠
◇ A Q 9 7 5	◇ 8 6 2	Pass	
♣ A 2	♣ K Q		

This time, East has a bad hand and no liking for diamonds, so signs off in 4♠ which West should respect.

This example illustrates the virtue of trial bids, but they may not always be the solution any more than Blackwood. Suppose that your hand was:

♠ A K 10 5 2
♡ 4 3 2
◇ A K Q J 5
♣ None

Again you open with 1♠ and are raised to 3♠. This time you don't want help in your second suit, which is already solid – what you want, purely and simply, is a control in hearts. Bidding 4◇ as a trial bid is useless, for you know that partner will have no help in diamonds and will sign off in 4♠ virtually whatever she has. This will be a pity, for facing:

♠ Q J 9 3
♡ A K 2
◇ 7 3
♣ J 10 9 7

seven spades is almost laydown, while opposite:

♠ Q J 9 3
♡ Q 7 5
◇ 10 4
♣ A Q 9 3

you may well lose the first three heart tricks in 5♠. What you want to do is to cue-bid 4♣ or 4◇ and hope to hear 4♡ from partner before proceeding – but you cannot do this, for four of a minor is a long suit trial bid.

Cue-bids or trial bids, then? Why not both! A modern idea is to use 3 NT in this type of auction to initiate a cue-bidding sequence, while a new suit directly is a trial bid. Now we can do this:

♠ A K 10 6 5	♠ Q J 9 3	1♠	3♠
♡ 4 3 2	♡ A K 2	3 NT[1]	4♡[2]
◇ A K Q J 5	◇ 7 3	5♣[2]	5♡[3]
♣ —	♣ J 10 9 7	5 NT[4]	6◇[5]
		7♠	Pass

[1] Starts cue-bidding sequence.
[2] Cue-bid, first-round control.
[3] Second-round heart control as well.
[4] Asking for top spades, as before.
[5] One high honour in spades.

♠ A K 10 6 5	♠ Q J 9 3	1♠	3♠
♡ 4 3 2	♡ Q 7 5	3 NT[1]	4♣[2]
◇ A K Q J 5	◇ 10 4	4◇[2]	4♠[3]
♣ —	♣ A Q 9 3	Pass	

[1] Starts cue-bidding sequence.
[2] Cue-bid, first-round control.
[3] No control in hearts.

This means giving up the use of 3 NT in the sequence:

1♠	3♠
3 NT	

as a natural bid. You should consider carefully whether this is worthwhile – if you play four-card majors and a weak no-trump, you may very well want to retain the natural meaning of 3 NT. My own view is that the ability to stop successfully in 3 NT when one of a major is raised to three is of little value compared with the much greater accuracy to be gained in slam bidding by using 3 NT to initiate cue-bids, but you must make up your own mind.

East's question concerning Blackwood was puzzling to Pat, who had not heard of one of the more useful variations on Blackwood to emerge in recent times. One of the problems with Blackwood is that it locates aces and kings wholesale, without reference to their location. Another is that it does not resolve the problem of the queen of trumps – often a crucial card in slam auctions.

Roman Key Card Blackwood

Roman Key Card Blackwood, usually abbreviated to RKCB, is a form of Blackwood designed to ensure not only that sufficient aces are held for a slam, but that the trump suit does not contain a gap. 4 NT is an asking bid, as before, but the responses count the king of the trump suit as a fifth ace and are:

5♣	No 'aces' or three 'aces'.
5♢	One or four 'aces'.
5♡	Two 'aces' without the queen of trumps.
5♠	Two 'aces' with the queen of trumps.
5 NT	Five 'aces'.

After a response of 5♣ or 5♢, the cheapest bid which is not the trump suit asks for the queen of trumps. Responder signs off without it or cue-bids an extra feature if the queen of trumps is held.

Here are some example hands:

♠ A K 10 5 2	♠ Q 9 6 4	1♠	3♠
♡ 3	♡ A 9 7 5	4 NT	5♠[1]
♢ A K Q 9 7	♢ J 2	7♠	Pass
♣ K 2	♣ A 5 4		

[1] Two aces and the queen of spades.

♠ A K 9 5 2	♠ 7 6 4 3	1♠	3♠
♡ 3	♡ A K 7 5	4 NT	5◇[1]
◇ A K Q 9 7	◇ J 2	5♡[2]	5♠[3]
♣ K 2	♣ Q 10 9	Pass	

[1] One ace.
[2] Do you have the queen of trumps?
[3] No.

Here, slam depends on a 2–2 trump break, which will happen only 40 per cent of the time, so is best avoided.

You may consider that the ambiguity of the 5♣ and 5◇ responses is a dangerous feature, but experience shows that this is not so. Before using Blackwood, you should have a very good idea from the preceding auction of your partner's strength, so you will be able to tell whether a 5♣ response contains no aces or three, and of course you should not use Blackwood if a response showing an inadequate number of aces will carry you too high. Still, there may arise circumstances where ambiguity exists – in such cases, the responder to Blackwood will carry on over partner's panic-stricken sign-off holding more aces than he might have! For example:

♠ K Q J 10 9 6	♠ A 7 4 3	1♠	4♠
♡ 2	♡ A 9 2	4 NT[1]	5♣[2]
◇ K Q J 10 9	◇ A 4 3	5♠[3]	6♠[4]
♣ 5	♣ 10 9 8	Pass[5]	

[1] RKCB – perhaps a trifle rash.
[2] No aces or three.
[3] Help! What have I done?
[4] Don't worry – I'm here to look after you.
[5] Thank goodness for that!

Post Mortem (continued)

Chris's reaction on seeing the bad trump break was purely human – he was so disgusted with the consequences of his impetuous bidding that he was in no state to apply his mind to the seemingly impossible task of avoiding a second trump loser. What West had seen and Chris had not, though, was that an opportunity existed for a trump endplay:

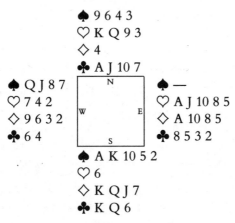

```
              ♠ 9 6 4 3
              ♡ K Q 9 3
              ◇ 4
              ♣ A J 10 7
♠ Q J 8 7         N        ♠ —
♡ 7 4 2                    ♡ A J 10 8 5
◇ 9 6 3 2    W        E    ◇ A 10 8 5
♣ 6 4                      ♣ 8 5 3 2
                 S
              ♠ A K 10 5 2
              ♡ 6
              ◇ K Q J 7
              ♣ K Q 6
```

After the two red aces and East's return of the ♡J, Chris, playing South, should have discarded a high club from his hand. A trump to South's ace is followed by three rounds of diamonds, throwing a heart and two clubs from the dummy. The ♣6 is led to dummy's ♣J and a heart is ruffed. The position is now:

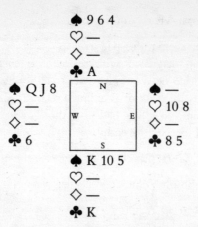

The ♣K is played to the ace, and the ♠9 run to West's ♠J. West is now endplayed, forced to lead from ♠Q 8 into declarer's ♠K 10, and declarer escapes for one down. No great triumph, to be sure – but it is vital at pairs to fight for every trick, and not simply to give up with downcast head when the going is tough.

Deal 2

Still kicking himself, Chris picked up his cards for the next deal:

North–South Vulnerable. Dealer West.

♠ A K J 9
♡ K J 9 2
♢ J 10 8 5
♣ 10

West opened briskly with one diamond, and Pat and East both passed. All this happened so quickly that Chris had barely finished sorting his hand before he had another awkward bidding decision to make.

'What now, I wonder?' he thought. 'I could double and hope that Pat bids a major suit, but what will happen if she bids clubs? I could bid a major of my own of course, but which one? Suppose I guess wrong and we end up playing in a 4–2 fit when we have a 4–4 fit in the other suit! Even one no-trump could be right – I have the values, but it runs a serious risk of missing a major suit fit. Maybe I should just pass, but that seems rather feeble. Why is life so difficult?'

What action would you take on Chris's hand?

Eventually, Chris decided to put his faith in the stronger of his two suits, and overcalled with one spade. West bid two clubs, which worried Chris for a moment since it now seemed that West and not Pat held the club suit. Maybe double would have been better after all.

'Stop, please' said Pat. 'Four spades.'

'I seem to have chosen well for a change,' thought Chris. His complacency was slightly disturbed, however, when East bid five clubs.

Chris's first instinct was to double, but despite the events of the first board he was still capable of rational thought. What tricks did he expect to take against five clubs, after all? West obviously had a lot of minor suit cards and East had few diamonds, so even two tricks was a lot to hope for and three was almost certainly out of the question unless Pat could double. 'Why did I not leave them in one diamond?' thought Chris as he passed.

West studied his hand for a while, then emerged with a bid which brought a gasp from Chris and sent Pat into a fit of choking. 'Five spades,' he said.

East, seemingly quite unperturbed, alerted by tapping the table. Pat, though, seemed bereft of the power of speech, and showed no inclination to ask East what West meant. She eventually managed a pass, and East gave matters fully five seconds consideration before making his call.

'Stop please – seven clubs,' he announced.

This was almost too much for Chris. A few moments ago, his opponents were in one diamond and he could have left them there. Now, they were in seven clubs and showed every sign that they knew exactly what they were doing. Still, it might be wise to ask what was going on.

'What did five spades mean?' he demanded of East.

'Well,' said the young man seriously, 'this sequence hasn't actually come up before. But I think that he has a good hand for his previous bidding, that he is confident that we can make six clubs, and that he feels we might make seven if I have any additional values.'

'Could he not have opened with something stronger than one diamond if that were the case?' persisted Chris.

'He can't open with a strong two in diamonds, if that's what

22

you mean' replied East. 'That would have a different meaning. He could have opened with a game-forcing two clubs, of course, but he might not have started with the high cards for that. His hand has obviously been improved by the club fit.'

'They clearly do know what they are doing,' thought Chris. 'Maybe I should sacrifice in seven spades. Let's see – we're vulnerable and they are not, so they will score 1440 if they make seven clubs. That means that I need to go five down or fewer in seven spades to show a profit. Well, Pat did raise to four spades, so I should be able to make eight tricks. Still, I looked ridiculous enough on the last deal. What will Pat say if I end up sacrificing in seven spades when I could have been defending one diamond?'

Would you take the vulnerable sacrifice in seven spades? Make up your mind before reading on.

'Pull yourself together,' Chris told himself sternly. 'The last board is history – concentrate on this one. Clearly the ace of spades is not going to take a trick against seven clubs. But my four diamonds, coupled with the fact that I have a singleton club, may get in declarer's way. Perhaps he will be unable to draw trumps and ruff out the diamonds. I think the best shot is to hope that seven clubs goes down – that way, we might score a top. If I sacrifice, we certainly won't score a great result and it might easily be a complete bottom.'

Chris eventually passed. Alas, the full deal was:

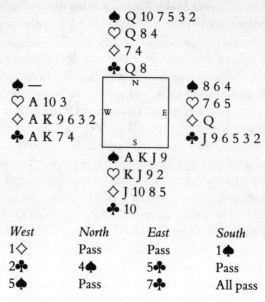

	North		
	♠ Q 10 7 5 3 2		
	♡ Q 8 4		
	◇ 7 4		
	♣ Q 8		

West
♠ —
♡ A 10 3
◇ A K 9 6 3 2
♣ A K 7 4

East
♠ 8 6 4
♡ 7 6 5
◇ Q
♣ J 9 6 5 3 2

South
♠ A K J 9
♡ K J 9 2
◇ J 10 8 5
♣ 10

West	North	East	South
1◇	Pass	Pass	1♠
2♣	4♠	5♣	Pass
5♠	Pass	7♣	All pass

West was able to make seven clubs with ease, needing only one diamond ruff in the dummy. Worse, it turned out that seven spades would have cost 1100 points only. There were some days, thought Chris to himself, when it just was not worth getting out of bed, and this certainly seemed to be one of them.

'You did well to bid seven,' said West to his partner.

'It was easy enough after five spades,' said East. 'Good bid, that.'

Everyone except Chris seemed to have forgotten that there had been a point at which the contract could have been one diamond. He spread his hand on the table mournfully. 'Was it so wrong to bid one spade?' he demanded of the Universe.

West gave the thirteen cards a cursory glance. 'Seems automatic,' he said. 'You can't pass, double feels wrong, and I don't like one no trump much.'

'Sure,' said East. 'And once you do bid, we're always going to bid the grand. Same auction at every table, I shouldn't wonder.'

Post Mortem

It was certainly reasonable, despite the unfortunate upshot, for Chris to bid something on the South hand. Since Pat had not overcalled, there was an inference that she did not have a five-card major with enough strength for North–South to make game, but there was no law against Pat having four hearts or four spades in a balanced twelve count or so.

If the South hand were given to an expert panel, there would probably be a number of votes for one spade, one heart, one no trump and double. Every one of that expert panel will at some stage have suffered in just the same way that Chris did on this hand. Once in a while, you will protect the opponents into a game or even a slam that they have failed to reach under their own steam. That does not mean that you should give up protective bidding – it simply means that as always in bridge, nothing works all the time.

Protective bidding

This is the name given to bidding by a player after a bid by his left hand opponent and two passes. It was originally called 'protective bidding' or 'protection', because the idea was that you were 'protecting' a pass from your partner that could have been made on fair values.

After West opens, North may have a reasonable hand but be unable to find a bid, since the requirements for an overcall are different from the requirements for an opening bid. Say that North holds:

♠ K 10 5 4
♡ A J 2
◇ Q 6 3
♣ A 5 4

and West opens one heart. There are those who would double, or bid one spade or even one no trump, but the hand falls some way short of the normal requirements for such actions. So North passes, as does East. Now South holds:

♠ Q J 6 3
♡ 10 3
◇ A 7 5
♣ Q 10 9 8

This is not a hand on which anyone would take action immediately over an opening bid of one heart. But if South tamely passes, West will be allowed to play in one heart and may well make it, while North–South can do quite nicely in two spades. So South doubles for takeout to *protect* his partner's pass.

Change the South hand slightly:

♠ Q J 6
♡ K 10 3
◇ A 7 5
♣ Q 10 9 8

Again, this is an obvious pass if one heart is opened on your right. But when it is opened on your left and followed by two passesd, you should once again *protect* your partner's pass – this time with one no-trump. Facing the example North hand, three no-trumps has every chance, so it will do you little good to defeat one heart by a trick or two.

You can see from this that the principles of protective bidding are fairly straightforward. If the opponents pass themselves out at a low level, but you do not have a great deal, the chances are that your partner has fair values but has been prevented from showing them by the opponents' bidding. Thus you make bids in the fourth seat, or *protective position*, that you would not make in the direct position.

A rule of thumb is that, for a protective action, you need about an ace less than you would for the same action in the direct position. To see this, take the two South hands given above and add an ace to each:

(1) ♠ Q J 6 3   (2) ♠ Q J 6
    ♡ 10 3   ♡ K 10 3
    ♢ A 7 5   ♢ A 7 5
    ♣ A Q 10 9   ♣ A Q 10 9

Now on hand (1) you would double one heart in the direct position, while on hand (2) you would overcall one no trump.

It follows from this that when partner is responding to your protective bid, she should simply pretend that her hand contains an ace less than it actually does, and bid what she would bid if that were the case. Thus on this North hand:

♠ K 10 5 4
♡ A J 2
♢ Q 6 3
♣ 7 5 4

you would raise an immediate overcall of one no-trump to three. Pretending that you have an ace less gives you a six count, though, with which you would pass an immediate overcall of one no-trump – so when your partner protects with one no-trump, you pass also.

The concept of protective bidding has these been extended to include positions where you are not so much protecting partner's immediate pass as protecting your own side's part-score contract. When the opponents bid:

West	East
1♡	2♡
Pass	

you know that (a) they have a heart fit, and (b) they have limited values. The fact that they have a heart fit increases the chance that your side has a fit also, and the fact that they have limited values makes it reasonably certain that your side has its fair share of high cards – indeed, you will often have more than the opponents.

Consider this hand:

♠ J 8 7 5 4
♡ 6 3
♢ A 7 2
♣ Q 8 6

You are North, and the auction proceeds:

West	North	East	South
1♡	Pass	2♡	Pass
Pass	?		

No guarantees, of course, but it is clearly right to bid two spades. Partner will have his fair shair of high cards, and is quite likely to have three or even four spades. This would be a typical hand:

♠ K 10 9
♡ A 5 4
♢ K J 6 5 4
♣ J 8

You may go down in two spades, of course, but that would be a little unlucky. Certainly, if you go down in two spades, the opponents were going to make two hearts, and at pairs scoring it makes a big difference whether you lose 50 on a deal or 110.

Because of the fact that, even if you protect and go down, at pairs you may still have done very well on the board, the tactics of protection are among the most vital areas of the pairs game. You should be sure that you and your partner are on the same wavelength, though. There are few experiences more trying than to protect delicately with two spades only to hear the man opposite raise you to four spades, doubled and two down.

Post mortem (continued)

Sometimes, of course, it all goes horribly wrong. Chris and Pat expected a bottom for this board, since East's assurance that the auction would be the same at every table did not seem particularly likely. In fact, the grand slam in clubs was bid at a few other tables, on the simple Acol auction:

West	East
2♢	2 NT
3♣	5♣
7♣	Pass

Two diamonds was strong, two no trumps a negative, and West's final call was not especially aggressive. Minus 1440 was not even a shared bottom, for at one table East–West bid to six clubs where they were doubled by South. The contract was promptly redoubled and made with an overtrick for the unusual score of 1580.

The Stop procedure
Pat's bid of four spades and East's final jump to seven clubs were both preceded by the words: 'Stop, please'. It is a rule of duplicate bridge that when a player is about to open at the two level or higher, or to make a bid that raises the level of the auction by more than five bids, the player must warn left hand opponent that this is going to happen.

The reason for this is that jump bids, which are very often pre-emptive in nature, can set a serious problem for the next hand to call. Suppose you hold this hand:

♠ K Q 9 5
♥ A J 4 3
♦ K 9 2
♣ A 4

You are all set to open one heart when, suddenly, the hand on your right opens the bidding with three diamonds. Now you have a problem, for it could be right to double or to overcall 3 NT, and you need time to think it over.

The trouble is, of course, that if you take this time, partner will be aware that you have a problem. If you decide to double, partner will know that your decision was not obvious, and that you do not have a hand like:

♠ K Q 9 5
♥ A J 4 3
♦ 7
♣ A Q 9 6

because that would be an automatic takeout double, which you would make without pause for thought.

Law 73C of the game says this: *When a player has available to him unauthorised information from his partner's remark, question, explanation, gesture, mannerism, special emphasis, inflection, haste or hesitation, he must carefully avoid taking any advantage that might accrue to his side.* And Law 16 says: *Players are authorised to base their actions on information from legal calls or plays, and from mannerisms of opponents. To base action on other, extraneous, information may be an infraction of law.*

What this means is that, although you are allowed all the time you need to think through a problem, your partner is not legally allowed to be aware that you had a problem, and must not base his own decisions on the fact that he knows you had a choice of actions. This is all very well in theory but, as I am sure you are aware, it is an extremely difficult practice to follow at the table.

Bids, especially pre-emptive bids, which raise the level of the auction unduly, are bound to create problems. In order partially to avoid the legal complications which arise, a warning is given before such a bid is made. The next player to call *must* pause, or 'Stop', for about ten seconds before making his call. He can use that time to think through the problem, and then when he makes a decision his partner will not have available any extraneous information.

West	North	East	South
'Stop – 2 NT'	Pass	'Stop – 6 NT'	All Pass

Clearly, in this auction, neither North nor South has many high cards and neither is likely to have any desire to do other than pass. Nevertheless, both must wait for ten seconds before doing so. A side effect of the procedure is to slow the game down, but its main effect is to make the game fairer for everyone. Please follow it at all times.

Please also be scrupulous about this. If you have a Yarborough and your right hand opponent opens three diamonds, it is *not* the done thing to fold your cards and ostentatiously look at your watch, counting off the statutory ten seconds, before you pass. That defeats the whole object, which is to protect you against conveying information to partner to which he is not entitled.

Deal 3

Chris was the picture of misery as his opponents left the table after the first round. All right, he had not bid well on the first board, but surely the second had been sheer bad luck. Something good had better happen soon, he told himself, or their chances of qualifying for the final would be zero. Not that they expected to qualify, of course – it was their first tournament, after all – but it would be nice not to finish last, and a few more boards like those two would leave precious little chance of that.

'Good afternoon,' said a voice from his left. Startled, he looked up to see the West chair occupied by a well-dressed middle-aged lady who was looking at him with mild concern. 'Are you all right?' she enquired kindly.

'What? Oh, yes, fine thanks,' said Chris. 'Sorry, I was just thinking.'

'Not a crime at a bridge tournament, at least not yet,' said the gentleman who had taken the seat on his right. He presented a neatly completed convention card for Chris's inspection, while his partner did the same for Pat. 'Acol, weak no-trump, multi two diamonds,' said East. 'And yourselves?'

'Just plain Acol,' broke in Pat. 'Weak no-trump, strong twos, nothing special.'

This was Pat's hand on the third board, vulnerable against not:

♠ A K 10 9 8 7
♡ 9 3 2
◇ Q J 5
♣ 3

Chris opened one heart, West passed and Pat bid one spade. East overcalled two clubs and Chris studied his hand for a while before emerging with three spades – prefixed, of course, by a warning to West that he was about to make a bid that required a ten-second pause.

'Stop, please,' said West after that time. 'Five clubs.'

'Typical,' thought Pat. 'This kind of bidding just doesn't happen at the club. I could have bid a nice four spades, probably made about eleven tricks and that would have been that. Now what? I guess I should bid five spades, but that might not make, or if Chris has just the right cards we could even have a slam. Surely I can't let them play five clubs, even doubled – we're vulnerable and they aren't going to go four down, so it must be right to bid.'

Make up your mind what you would do with Pat's hand before reading on.

There comes a time when every bridge player believes that she or he needs to do something to alter the course of destiny. Pat knew that she and Chris had had an awful start to the competition, and felt that it was time to make a stand.

'If I bid six spades confidently,' she said to herself, 'maybe these opponents will believe I mean it. They aren't vulnerable and they have a big club fit, so it's possible that even if we can't make six spades – and I doubt that we can – they may sacrifice in seven clubs. In any case, one more bottom won't matter. It's a top we need now, and there's only one way to get one.'

Pat's bid of six spades took the whole table by surprise. East passed in an even tempo, Chris passed apprehensively, and West thought for a very long time. 'Good,' thought Pat to herself, 'she must be thinking of a sacrifice.' But West finally passed, and Pat awaited the dummy with no little trepidation.

East led the ace of clubs, and Chris spread his dummy:

♠ A K 10 9 8
♡ 9 3 2
♢ Q J 5
♣ 3

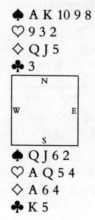

♠ Q J 6 2
♡ A Q 5 4
♢ A 6 4
♣ K 5

'Good luck,' said Chris. 'Maybe two spades would have been safer.'

'Thank you,' said Pat, trying to sound confident and almost succeeding.

East continued with a second round of clubs. Pat won dummy's king and, before discarding from her hand, went into a long trance. What line of play would you adopt?

This was the full deal:

North–South game.
Dealer South.

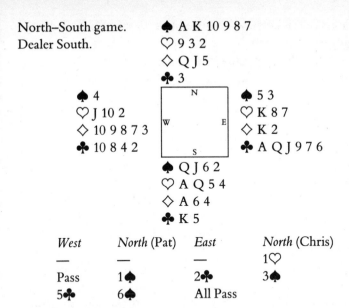

♠ A K 10 9 8 7
♡ 9 3 2
♢ Q J 5
♣ 3

♠ 4
♡ J 10 2
♢ 10 9 8 7 3
♣ 10 8 4 2

N
W E
S

♠ 5 3
♡ K 8 7
♢ K 2
♣ A Q J 9 7 6

♠ Q J 6 2
♡ A Q 5 4
♢ A 6 4
♣ K 5

West	North (Pat)	East	North (Chris)
—	—	—	1♡
Pass	1♠	2♣	3♠
5♣	6♠	All Pass	

Pat's first thought was that the contract was hopeless. Even if the heart finesse and the diamond finesse both succeeded, she would still have a loser in one of the red suits (the other loser could be discarded on the king of clubs, of course). Maybe she should throw a heart on the king of clubs, then play for East to have the singleton king of diamonds. This seemed horribly unlikely, though – was there no other hope?

Suddenly she saw it, and began to play with confidence and speed. She discarded a heart on the king of clubs, drew trumps with the seven and eight to show off, and finessed dummy's queen of hearts. She cashed dummy's ace of hearts and ruffed a heart, setting up the thirteenth card in dummy as a master. Next, she led the queen of diamonds which East covered with the king. Winning with dummy's ace, Pat threw her losing diamond on the last heart and claimed the rest of the tricks.

'Well done!' said Chris. Maybe life was not so bad after all.

'Well done indeed,' said West graciously, 'but you needed a

few things to go well for you. I should have saved in seven clubs, partner.'

'How does that go?' mused East aloud. 'One spade, two hearts, two diamonds and a club – six down. Only 1400, as opposed to 1430. Most remiss of you, my dear.'

Post Mortem

Some of the most uncomfortable decisions in bridge – especially at pairs – have to be taken at the five level. The opponents, trading on the favourable vulnerability, will not let you play in a comfortable four of a major. They will bounce you to the five level before you have a chance to exchange information, and force you to guess.

At other forms of scoring, this guess is not so important. Nobody ever went broke collecting 500 instead of a game at rubber bridge, and at teams scoring the loss is only three international match points (IMPs) compared with the twelve that you lose if you bid on and are wrong. So, if the form of scoring is anything other than pairs, players are inclined to simply 'take the money'. At pairs, though, it is different. If you collect 500 when the rest of the field scores 650, you will get a bottom, which makes the pressure to bid on far more acute.

Here, West made a typical pressure bid of five clubs, and Pat faced an awkward decision. It was almost certain, after Chris's bid of three spades, that her side could make a vulnerable game. Moreover, since she had six spades and Chris had promised four, there was no chance of more than one spade trick in defence and quite possibly none at all. The rest of Pat's hand contained very little in the way of defensive values, so there was practically no chance that the penalty from five clubs would be adequate. (In fact, five clubs costs 800, but this is largely due to the miracle lie of cards which allows six spades to make.) It would therefore have been entirely normal for Pat to continue to five spades, producing the standard result on the deal.

The forcing pass

This is a topic on which whole books can be (and have been) written, so I will deal with it only briefly here. In situations such as this, where it is clear that the enemy are sacrificing, it may well be that the player directly to speak after the sacrifice bid does not have a clear course of action. With a clear preference for defending, you can double. With a clear preference for bidding on, you can do so. But if your hand is neither one thing nor the other, you can leave the decision to partner by simply passing. This is 'forcing' in the sense that partner cannot pass – but he was never going to do that anyway, so to refer to a 'forcing pass' in this type of position is merely giving a grandiose name to a piece of common sense. Bridge players are quite fond of doing that.

Suppose that Pat's hand had been:

> ♠ A K 10 9 4
> ♡ K 3 2
> ◇ K 5 3
> ♣ 3 2

for the auction above. Now five spades might lose three tricks, especially if partner had a small doubleton club also, while five clubs doubled could easily cost 800 if five spades were making. As against that, Pat's hand has more playing strength than a response of one spade to one heart might contain, so it could be that 650 in five spades would be preferable to 500 or so from five clubs.

This is, in short, a typical hand where the forcing pass is useful, saying in effect: 'We might make five spades, but only if you have some reserves of playing strength for your bidding. If so, I won't mind if you bid on – if not, please double.'

In what circumstances does a forcing pass exist? You and your partner should discuss this question carefully, for it is an area in which there is considerable disagreement even among the world's top experts. The vast majority of them would agree, though, that a forcing pass is available if this condition is met: our side is bidding 'constructively' and the enemy 'pre-emptively'. In the auction on this deal, Chris and opened and Pat had responded, then Chris had shown extra values and a fit with his raise to three spades. The opponents had overcalled and then jumped to the five level, almost certainly as a sacrifice, so the above condition had clearly been met.

You can extend the principle in a number of ways:

West	North	East	South
3◇	Double	5◇	?

West has opened with a pre-emptive bid, North's double is a constructive move denoting a good hand, and East has jumped to an awkward level. Suppose South holds this hand:

♠ A J 4 3
♡ K Q 6 5
◇ 3 2
♣ Q 3 2

You may be well advised to defend five diamonds doubled, which is likely to go down – but this could be a poor score if you can make five or even six of either major. The trouble is that if you plunge into five hearts or five spades, you could find yourself in a 4–3 fit going down, which would be a horrible result. It would be a good idea to pass and see what partner thinks – but you can only do that if pass is forcing, for defending five diamonds undoubled will not be a good score!

Therefore, on the basis that our side has made a constructive call while the opponents are pre-empting, many experts would treat a pass here as forcing. That may strike you as a little advanced or even a little dangerous, but the important thing is for you to be aware of the possibilities even if you decide that some of them are not for you.

Of course, just as in every aspect of bridge, there is nothing that works all the time. It has occasionally happened to every expert that he or she is in a 'forcing pass position' where the alternatives are to double the opponents for −790 or to bid on for −800! You pay a price for every convention that you play, but experience has shown the forcing pass to be a most valuable weapon − provided, as always, that both members of the partnership are on the same wavelength.

Post Mortem (continued)

Pat's actual bid of six spades is not commended as an example of bridge judgment. The contract is not very likely to make, and opponents are not pressured into a sacrifice as often as people like to think that they are when making bids of this nature.

Estimating your score
For all the above, it is certainly the case that in the pairs game, you sometimes need to create a little of your own luck. Taking a wild action may well be the only sensible thing to do − if you can gauge that you need a top to qualify for a final, or win a big prize, there is no point in taking the sober decision that will get you an average. If a session is not going well, you may have time to turn it around should you bid and make a lucky game or slam − if you go down, it wasn't going to be your session anyway.

To this end, it is important to develop a feeling for how well or badly things are going during a session. Most good pairs players can guess to within a couple of percentage points their score on a particular board, and very many of them keep a running total of these estimates. The method is simple − on the score card after each result, they write a figure from zero to ten which represents an estimate of their score. Zero is a bottom, five is an average, ten is a top. It does not matter what the real top on the board is going to be − at the end of the session, there is a column of figures which can be added and converted to the estimated percentage score for the session.

So far, it has not been diffcult to estimate the scores for Chris and Pat. The first board was horrible, and will be lucky to score one out of ten. The second was unlucky, but other pairs might achieve the same result, so it can be given two out of ten. This board is going to be a top, or very near it – perhaps some other Norths will be inspired or crazy enough to come up with Pat's bid of six spades, but it seems highly unlikely. Chris, at any rate, wrote down ten with a flourish in the column where he records his estimates.

Thirteen out of thirty for our heroes, then – not brilliant, but a start on the road to recovery. Remember that they are going to need about 55 per cent to qualify for the final, and they are going to play twenty-four boards in the qualifying session. When it is all over, then, Chris's estimates will need to add up to around 132. Starting with the next board, we will keep a check on how they are doing.

Post Mortem (continued)

'Whatsoever a man soweth, that shall he also reap,' said Paul to the Galatians, who were not bridge players and would not have understood him had he written: 'If you bid rotten contracts, you have to play them well.' Pat's bidding may not be above criticism, but her play was very fine. The tactic of discarding a loser in a suit where you have length rather than shortage is well known, but strangely easy to miss, especially when you are in a state of panic at your own bidding. Of course, not all of those finesses had to work, and the heart suit did not have to divide 3–3, but a slim chance is always better than none and Pat did very well to play calmly for her only shot.

As an exercise, how would you plan the play in 4♠ on this pair of hands?

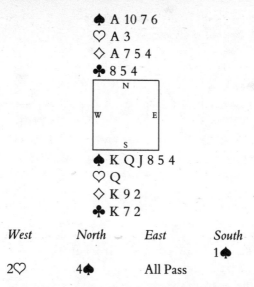

♠ A 10 7 6
♡ A 3
♢ A 7 5 4
♣ 8 5 4

♠ K Q J 8 5 4
♡ Q
♢ K 9 2
♣ K 7 2

West	North	East	South
			1♠
2♡	4♠	All Pass	

West leads the ♠9 to which East follows. On a second round of trumps, West discards the ♡J and East follows suit.

This is not a great contract, for West is likely to hold the ♣A for his overcall, and you are in danger of losing a diamond and three clubs should East obtain the lead. A possibility would be to win the second spade in dummy and lead a low diamond, hoping that East will play low and you will be able to insert the ♢9. West cannot attack clubs with profit, and you may later be able to discard a club loser on the long diamond if the suit should divide 3–3. Is there anything better?

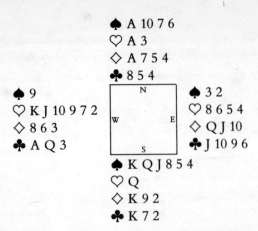

♠ A 10 7 6
♡ A 3
◇ A 7 5 4
♣ 8 5 4

♠ 9
♡ K J 10 9 7 2
◇ 8 6 3
♣ A Q 3

♠ 3 2
♡ 8 6 5 4
◇ Q J 10
♣ J 10 9 6

♠ K Q J 8 5 4
♡ Q
◇ K 9 2
♣ K 7 2

As you can see, even if East is asleep you will simply not be able to duck a diamond to West, and East should have no difficulty in playing a club through on winning the third diamond trick. Can you see the answer, bearing in mind Pat's play on the deal above?

At the third trick, lead the ♡Q from your hand – and duck in dummy when West covers with the ♡K! West may as well continue with a second heart and you win dummy's ♡A, discarding a diamond from your hand. Cash the ◇K and ◇A, ruff a diamond, return to dummy with a spade and discard a losing club on the long diamond. If the diamonds do not break, of course, you will still have the chance of playing a club towards the king for your tenth trick.

Deal 4

'That was lucky!' said Pat impulsively.

'Yes,' said her partner, who knew that there was another board to be played against the same opponents and that it was not done to gloat. 'Could you put the next board on the table, please?'

'Sorry,' said Pat, but if East and West resented her display of pleasure at her good fortune, they did not show it. This was Chris's hand as South on the fourth deal:

Game All. Dealer West.
♠ K J 6 5
♡ K J 6
♢ K 6
♣ K J 8 5

West and North both passed and East opened one spade, leaving Chris with a delicate decision. What would you do in his position?

'I have the high cards for an overcall of one no-trump,' Chris thought, 'but only just. And this is really not as good a hand as it looks – no aces, no intermediates, less chance of a fit for us after that opening bid. I honestly don't think it can be right to bid here, especially vulnerable. It's just too likely that we'll go down, possibly doubled, while the opponents can't make very much at all. Besides, if there is a contract on for us, partner still has another chance, and judging by the last hand she has decided to make as many bids as she can for the entry fee.'

43

'Pass,' said Chris, hoping that he had not given too much indication that he was close to a bid. That might make it difficult for Pat to protect on a marginal hand.

But neither West nor Pat had any interest in proceeding further, so Chris had his second awkward decision in as many minutes – what should he lead? Make your choice before reading on .

'I wish I'd bid now,' thought Chris to himself. 'What an awful hand to lead from! They say that you should never lead away from a king against a suit contract, but if I were to follow that rule it might be some time before we could start the next round. I'm not going to lead the king of diamonds – that's just wild. A trump could be safe, but it might not, and anyway it will only postpone the decision. No, it's a heart or a club, but which?'

Can you see any reason for preferring either suit? Chris continued his musing: 'Whichever I lead, if partner has the ace or queen we're probably OK. If declarer has both the ace and queen, I've blown it. But if declarer has the ace and dummy the queen, or the other way round, it may be better to lead the shorter suit, since the opponents are more likely to have length there so it may not give away a trick that won't come back. I hate it, but I'm going to lead a heart.'

This was the full deal: Game all. Dealer West.

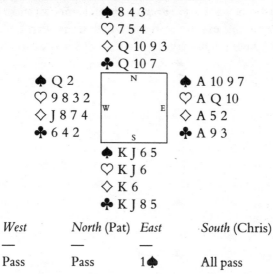

	♠ 8 4 3	
	♡ 7 5 4	
	◇ Q 10 9 3	
	♣ Q 10 7	

West	North (Pat)	East	South (Chris)
—	—	—	
Pass	Pass	1♠	All pass

Dummy went down with nothing in hearts, but nothing in clubs either, and Chris held his breath to see what the result of his choice would be. When Pat could only furnish the four of hearts and declarer won the trick with the ten, Chris had to fight the urge to groan in dismay. East studied his prospects for some while, then shrugged and played the ace and queen of hearts, leaving Chris back on lead again.

'Well,' he thought, 'that's torn it. I've given away a heart trick, and here I am back on lead with not much more idea about what to do than I had when I started. I think I must hope that a club lead would have been equally bad for our side, so I am not going to lead one now. What was it that Frenchman said? ' "*Mon centre cède, ma droite récule, situation excellente! J'attaque!*" '

With as much insouciance as he could find (which was not very much), Chris tossed out the king of diamonds. East won the ace and returned the suit hopefully, but when Chris played low declarer played low from dummy also. This was well reasoned by East – surely Chris would not have led a heart from ♡K J 6 if he had the king and queen of diamonds, and there might be some value in keeping the jack in dummy. Pat, who had been wool-gathering, won the trick with the nine to leave this position:

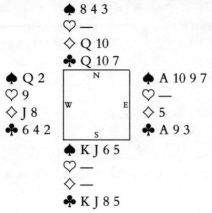

```
                    ♠ 8 4 3
                    ♡ —
                    ◇ Q 10
                    ♣ Q 10 7
     ♠ Q 2                        ♠ A 10 9 7
     ♡ 9              N           ♡ —
     ◇ J 8      W         E       ◇ 5
     ♣ 6 4 2                      ♣ A 9 3
                    S
                    ♠ K J 6 5
                    ♡ —
                    ◇ —
                    ♣ K J 8 5
```

It seemed to Pat that her partner had been strangely reluctant to lead either black suit, and that declarer was following a very passive line. Maybe East had something like ♣K J 9, in which case a club return would only help his cause. There appeared to be no harm in a trump return, since this would give declarer nothing that was not his in any case. To her partner's chagrin, she played not a club but a spade.

Declarer played low and Chris won with the king. Now, though, he was aware that declarer had the ◇A and the ♡A Q, and presumably the ♠A also, he could not hold the ace and queen of clubs since this would give him a balanced twenty count and he would probably have opened 2 NT. Regretting that he had not led the traditional fourth highest card of his longest suit at trick one, Chris finally switched to a small club to the queen and ace. Declarer crossed to the queen of spades and led the nine of hearts from dummy in this position, needing two more tricks for his contract:

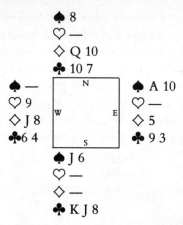

Pat ruffed with the eight of spades, declarer threw a small club, and Chris was just about to do likewise when he paused to reflect. Doubtless, Pat had the queen of diamonds and could cash that card next, but the position would then be:

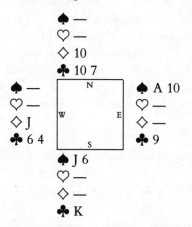

Whatever North did now, East was bound to score both his ace and ten of spades to make the contract. Replacing the eight of clubs in his hand, Chris discarded the jack of that suit instead.

East glanced sharply at his left hand opponent. He had played a fairly hopeless contract with considerable skill to give himself a chance, and the defence until now had been less than perfect, but it seemed that the young man in the South seat had found the resources to thwart him at the last. Pat cashed the queen of diamonds, East followed suit, Chris threw the king of clubs and East smiled warmly at him. Pat, to Chris's great relief, produced the ten of clubs to which all followed, and was left on play to lead through declarer's ace-ten of spades at the twelfth trick. One down.

'Well defended!' said East sportingly.

'Some of the time, anyway,' said Chris, with a grateful laugh.

Port Mortem

Chris's decision not to overcall the opening one spade with one no-trump was a good one. He had the required 15 points, and he certainly had the spade suit well stopped, but his hand was short of playing strength and well suited for defence. If his side could score a small plus score playing the hand, it might well be that one spade could be defeated by two tricks for 200 points, better than any part-score for North–South. If, on the other hand, the deal belonged to the opponents, then a risky overcall might easily give them the chance to extract 200 points or more themselves.

The magic 200

Reference is often made in books and articles to 'the magic 200' at pairs scoring. This is because, if the deal is a part-score, any side which scores plus 200 will do very well – a magic result. Good pairs players are always careful to avoid actions which could result in 200 to the opponents, while seeking every opportunity to obtain that score for their own side. The vulnerability is critical in these cases. If the opponents are vulnerable, it is usually better to let them play their contract and hope for 200 – perhaps doubling aggressively for one down – while if they are not vulnerable and it does not seem very likely that they will be two down, it is usually better to compete for your own side's best part-score contract.

Post Mortem (continued)

The reasoning which induced Chris to start with a heart lead rather than a club was not without logic, but was probably unsound. A very good principle is that, if you have length in trumps, you should generally attempt to force declarer to use his trumps by ruffing, so that your length in the suit will come into its own. To that end, it is better to attack with your long suits rather than with short ones. If you give away a trick by force of high cards, there is still a good chance that you will recoup the trick through causing declarer to run out of trumps – the 'forcing game', as it is called. The reason that 'fourth highest of your longest and strongest' is a bridge axiom which has survived the test of time better than any other is that it works.

On this deal, the fact that a club lead is miles better than a heart, has more to do with good fortune than good sense. The opening lead is the riskiest part of the game, especially when there has been little bidding to guide you to the right choice. For that reason, it is good strategy at pairs to resolve difficult choices in favour of what you think the rest of the players with your cards will do. If your decision works poorly, so will theirs.

East, as we have seen, played the contract very well to give himself a chance. His trump holding was such that it would clearly be better if the opponents could be forced to lead it – or led it by mistake – and by skilful reasoning and passive play he actually succeeded in establishing two potential winners in dummy, the ♡9 and the ◇J. He could not hope to cash either, of course, but their mere presence had a telling effect on his play.

The reasoning that led Chris to find the dramatic switch to the king of diamonds at the fourth trick was interesting. It is often the case that, when your opening lead turns out poorly, you should hope that the alternative would have been equally poor, so that you are no worse off than the rest of the field. On this deal, though, South was quite likely to be faced with unattractive choices at several stages during the play, and it would have been better strategy simply to get the club suit over and done with.

For all that, no harm came of the diamond switch. Pat's play of a spade rather than a club at the sixth trick was a mistake, but at least she had a reason for it and it gave her partner a chance to be brilliant in the end game. That kind of mistake is more easily forgiven than most.

The score

At some tables, South had chosen to overcall one no-trump after the opening one spade by East. That worked well in some cases, for South managed to come to eight tricks at a couple of tables and to seven at another – but East, seduced by his eighteen card points (HCPs), had doubled. This crazy decision received slightly more than its due reward: two match points instead of none.

At other tables, South took seven tricks only in one no-trump. This came about in one case because West hit on the good lead of the two of spades rather than the queen. East won the ace and returned the ten, South, not unnaturally (though mistakenly) finessed the jack, and West was able to put his queen to good use. The defenders took three spade tricks and three aces. It is often excellent play to lead low, rather than the honour, from a doubleton honour in partner's suit against no-trumps, especially if you have good reason to believe that declarer will hold the stoppers.

At the tables where one spade was the final contract, it was defeated on a club lead almost all the time. One East player had made the contract on muddled defence, and one had gone two down through muddled play.

This meant that Chris and Pat scored almost an exact average for plus 100, beating the plus 90s and the minus 80 their way, tying with the other plus 100s, and losing to the plus 120s, the 180 and the 200. Chris felt that he deserved more for his ingenious unblock in clubs, but reflected later that maybe that heart lead had not been such a great idea after all.

Finesses and when to avoid them

An astonishing number of players have a blind spot when faced with this combination of cards:

♠ A J 4 3   ♠ K 6 5

Requiring three tricks from the suit, declarers will blithely cash the king, then finesse the jack. East wins with the queen, but our heroes do not despair for there is still the chance that the suit will divide 3–3. When East proves to have started with a doubleton queen, the Souths shrug their shoulders and proceed to the next hand, totally unaware that they have made a hash of this one.

Of course, the correct play for three tricks in the suit is to cash the ace, then the king, then lead towards dummy's remaining ♠J 4. If you think about it for a moment, you will see that this line wins three tricks *whenever it is possible to do so*. It will never win four tricks, of course, and since overtricks are important at pairs scoring it may be that you will feel, next time you are faced with the combination, that you do not wish to give up the overtrick when West has ♠Q x x in order to insure against East having the (slightly less likely) ♠Q x. We will discuss the question of when to play for overtricks and when to play safe later in the book, but the pitfall of the premature finesse occurs far more often than most players believe, and it is as well to be on your guard.

Take the South who played in 1 NT against a low spade lead

on the deal above. The spade suit, you will recall, was:

♠ 8 4 3

♠ Q 2   ♠ A 10 9 7

♠ K J 6 5

When East won the first spade and returned the suit, it was perhaps human nature for South to finesse, and West gained his reward for his inspired (though technically correct) lead. But South had nothing to gain by taking the finesse! If West had started with a singleton ♠2, South's ♠J 6 would still be a trick later in the play.

Suppose that this is your trump suit:

♠ A Q 4 3   ♠ 9 6 5 2

Would you start to draw trumps with a finesse of the ♠Q? Think again – then start by cashing the ♠A instead. You can later lead up to the ♠Q, and if West has the king once or twice guarded, you have lost nothing. If East has the *guarded* ♠K, you will lose two tricks, of course – but you would have lost those anyway by finessing the ♠Q. But if East has the *singleton* ♠K . . .

There is, as it happens, a still better way to tackle that trump suit. Try leading a small card *away* from dummy on the first round. Now, if East has the king and one other card – not the jack, of course – he may feel that he has a problem. It is a purely imaginary problem, for you would not be tackling the suit in this way if you actually held the ♠J or a five-card suit, so East ought to play low smoothly. But how many Easts do you know who would do that every time? If the answer to this is 'several', then you play in company so exalted that this book is probably not for you.

Most of the time, the king will not appear on the first round of trumps when you lead low from dummy. If it does not, you have lost nothing, for you can always finesse the ♠A Q on the next round. Study the position carefully to convince yourself that this is so.

Experts hate finesses, and will go to great lengths to avoid them – some technical, some psychological. If you want to focus on a single point to improve your declarer play, then you could do a lot worse than concentrate on this question: before I take the finesse that I am about to take, is there any way in which I can do better by avoiding it?

Deal 5

The previous round had taken a little more than the allocated fifteen minutes, and the Tournament Director was standing behind Chris's chair. 'You're a bit behind time,' he said. 'Try to catch up on this round, please.'

'It's all very well for him to talk,' thought Chris. 'He doesn't have to find brilliant jettisons of high cards to prevent trump endplays – these things take time, you know.'

But Chris was conscious of the fact that if a pairs tournament is to run smoothly and fairly for all the competitors, it is essential that the official rate of play – fifteen minutes for each two-board round – is maintained. He apologized to the Tournament Director and to his new opponents, who were quick to reassure him.

'Don't worry,' said the bearded youth who had taken the West seat. 'We're very fast players, there'll be no problem catching up.'

'Not very good, mind you,' said the bespectacled sixteen-year-old in the East position. 'Just very fast.'

Pat and Chris both laughed, but somehow Pat felt that the young man on her left was being a trifle over-modest. Both opponents had convention cards covered with a mass of writing, and both looked very much as though they knew what they were doing. She picked up her hand for the fifth board, on which she was the dealer:

♠ A Q
♡ A 9 8 5
♢ A 8 7 2
♣ Q 10 3

'One heart,' she said, trying to sound as confident as her opponents looked.

East passed, and Chris bid two diamonds which gave Pat something of a problem. What would you rebid on her hand?

'I'd like to support diamonds, obviously,' thought Pat. 'But three diamonds would be a bit feeble with sixteen points – I might do that on eleven or twelve. What about four diamonds? That's better in terms of showing extra values, but it takes us past three no trumps, which could easily be our best contract.'

Pat made up her mind. 'Two no trumps,' she said, feeling that this bid expressed the nature of her hand better than any other. If necessary, she would support diamonds strongly in the later auction, but for now it seemed best to show the balanced nature of her hand and its strength.

Chris raised to three no trumps, however, so there was no question of supporting diamonds any more. Everyone passed, and East turned to Chris.

'Two no trumps forcing, was it?' he enquired.

'Not that I'm aware of,' said Chris, puzzled. 'It shows about 15–17 and a balanced hand. I can pass if I want – we just play simple Acol.'

'Thank you,' said East politely, and he led the two of hearts. Pat studied her problem:

♠ A Q
♡ A 9 8 5
♢ A 8 7 2
♣ Q 10 3

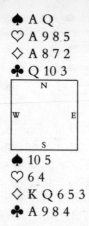

♠ 10 5
♡ 6 4
♢ K Q 6 5 3
♣ A 9 8 4

'Rather minimum, I'm afraid,' said Chris. 'Perhaps I should have passed, but . . .'

Pat was not listening. She played dummy's four of hearts and West contributed the king. How would you plan the play?

A brief glance at her opponents' convention card revealed that they played fourth highest leads, so it seemed that the heart suit was not a threat. The spade suit certainly was, however – if Pat ducked the first heart, West might switch to a spade through the ♠A Q, with dire consequences. With this in mind, Pat won the first trick and considered her prospects.

'Assuming the diamonds break,' she mused, 'I have eight tricks on top. The spade finesse might work, but I'm only going to take that if I absolutely have to. It looks better to play on clubs. I can take two finesses against East by running the queen, then the ten. If he has the decency to hold either the king or the jack – or both – I'll make three club tricks and it will all be plain sailing.'

Pat cashed the ♢K and ♢A, to which both opponents followed. Next she led the queen of clubs, but East played low imperturbably. The first flicker of doubt began to occupy Pat's mind, but she was committed to running the ♣Q. West took the trick with the king, cashed the ♡J followed by the ♡10, and – of course – switched to the spade that Pat had been dreading. The position now was:

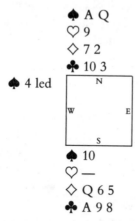

```
              ♠ A Q
              ♡ 9
              ◇ 7 2
              ♣ 10 3
  ♠ 4 led    ┌─────────┐
             │    N    │
             │W       E│
             │    S    │
             └─────────┘
              ♠ 10
              ♡ —
              ◇ Q 6 5
              ♣ A 9 8
```

East still had the ♡Q, so if Pat finessed the spade and it lost her opponent would cash the heart trick for one down. Alternatively, she could go up with the ♠A and take a second finesse in clubs, which would bring in the rest of the tricks if it succeeded and almost certainly lose all but one of the rest of the tricks if it did not. How would you play in this position?

'Don't panic,' Pat told herself. 'Which finesse should I take – spades or clubs? I started with a 75 per cent chance that East would have one of the club honours, but now that West has turned up with the ♣K I'm fairly sure it's an even chance who has the ♣J. What about the ♠K – is that an even chance also?

'East led the ♡2 and we know that he started with four to the queen. If he had five spades, he would surely have led one, so I must assume that West has at least five spades to East's four. That makes West a 5–4 on favourite to hold any particular spade, especially in this case the ♠K. Besides, if East had started with ♠K x x x and ♡Q x x x, might he not have preferred to lead from his stronger suit – a spade, rather than a heart?

'I think that I must take the spade finesse after all. It might be wrong, but at least I will go only one down as opposed to thousands down if I go up with the ♠A and lose a club finesse.'

Suiting her actions to her thoughts, Pat played the ♠Q and closed her eyes. When she opened them again, the ♠Q had held the trick, for this was the full deal:

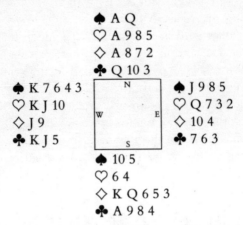

Pat had nine tricks now, but there seemed little risk in trying for a tenth by running the ♣10. When West took this trick with the jack, Pat's relief was complete – if she had rejected the spade finesse in favour of the second club finesse, the carnage would have been frightful. As it was, she had made her contract, a fact which she hastened to record on the travelling score sheet.

'Well done,' said West. 'Close to going an awful lot down there, weren't you? Still, you played with the odds.'

'They do know what they're doing,' thought Pat. 'Better be careful on the next deal.'

Chris had not been paying attention to the play, but if his opponents were congratulating his partner she must have done something clever. 'Yes, good effort partner,' he said, looking for all the world as if he knew what he was talking about. 'Definitely the percentage line.'

Post Mortem

Pat's many problems on this deal started with her rebid after 1♡–2◇. Her decision to bid 2 NT was entirely correct for a number of reasons. First, it is almost always a good idea to limit your hand in terms of type – balanced or unbalanced – and strength as early as you can in the auction. 2 NT achieved this purpose, showing a balanced hand in the range 15–17.

Second, when your side has unearthed a minor suit fit and the values for game, it is usually wise to head not for five of the minor, but for 3 NT. You need substantial extra values to make eleven tricks in the suit contract, while you will often find that you need less than the 'statutory' 25 points for 3 NT if you have a minor suit that you can run for five or six tricks. Of course, it may become clear from the bidding that your side lacks a stopper in a particular suit, or that your tricks will come from a cross-ruff in the minor suit game, in which case 3 NT should be avoided (it is difficult to make 3 NT on a cross-ruff!). In general, though, major suit fits play game in four of the major, but minor suit fits play game in 3 NT.

This argument applies to all forms of bridge, but especially to the pairs game. It is no use making eleven tricks in five diamonds, scoring 600, when you could have made ten in 3 NT for 630. Even if the minor suit game plays two tricks better than 3 NT, a score of 620 will still bring in zero match points if the field is scoring 630.

That is why you will see players stretch to bid minor suit slams – they realise that once they have gone past 3 NT, their best chance for a good pairs score is that the minor suit contract will make twelve tricks and they can collect the slam bonus. I do not advocate that you join their ranks, for it is depressing to bid slams that do not make. But I do suggest that if the early rounds of bidding disclose a minor suit fit in your hands, you should direct later efforts towards 3 NT rather than five of the minor.

The forcing 2 NT rebid

East's question concerning the forcing nature of the sequence:

$$1\heartsuit \qquad 2\diamondsuit$$
$$2\,NT$$

puzzled Chris, but a standard expert treatment is to play this rebid as forcing. This is not even a 'convention' as such, since it arises from the logic of the bidding. A two-level response to a one-level opening normally shows a minimum of 9 points, very often more. A 2 NT rebid shows a minimum of 15 points. So, by the time we have bid:

$$1\heartsuit \qquad 2\diamondsuit$$
$$2\,NT$$

we have already established that we hold at the *very least* 24 points between us, and usually more. In other words, we are at worst extremely close to having the values for game, and 99 times out of 100 we will have comfortably enough. So, we want the bidding to continue beyond 2 NT and it makes sense to regard the bid as forcing.

What are the advantages? First, certain 'awkward' hand types become less so:

♠ K J 8 6 5	♠ A Q 3
♡ A K 3	♡ J 5
◇ 7 6	◇ 8 3 2
♣ A K 5	♣ Q J 10 9 8
1♠	2♣
?	

West has no idea what the best contract is going to be here. The point count suggests a jump to 3 NT, but that could be crazy if partner has three-card support for spades and a weakness in diamonds. How will he know to convert to 4♠ – after all, we could have only four of those and the red suits well stopped. Should West, then, jump to 3♠? Possibly, but this rebid really ought to show a much better suit than ♠K J 8 6 5 – something like ♠A Q J 10 9 3 would be closer to the mark.

The solution is for West to rebid 2 NT, confident that East will not pass. On the deal above, the auction would be:

1♠	2♣
2 NT (forcing)	3♠
4♠	Pass

Suppose the East hand were different:

♠ K J 8 6 5	♠ A 3
♡ A K 3	♡ J 5
♦ 7 6	♦ K 8 3 2
♣ A K 5	♣ Q J 10 9 8

1♠	2♣
2 NT (forcing)	3♦
3 NT	Pass

Or even:

♠ K J 8 6 5	♠ A 3
♡ A K 3	♡ Q J 10 9
♦ 7 6	♦ 8 3
♣ A K 5	♣ Q J 10 9 8

1♠	2♣
2 NT (forcing)	3♡
4♡!	Pass

This last auction looks like a conjuring trick, but I assure you I have nothing up my sleeve. West does not have four hearts when he rebids 2 NT. Why not? Because if he had five spades and four hearts, he would rebid 2♡. If he had four spades and four hearts, he would open 1♡. So, why might East bid hearts?

Either he has five – in which case West should assuredly raise them – or he has four and is concerned about diamonds. West shares this concern, realizes that 3 NT is out, and offers East a choice of 4♡, 4♠ and 5♣ as possible game contracts. East knows that 4♡ is a 4–3 fit, but he also knows that it will be a good contract. If you play a 2 NT rebid as forcing, you too can have magic auctions like this.

A further advantage of the forcing 2 NT rebid is that it enables you to distinguish between hand types when supporting partner. Suppose you open 1♠ and partner bids 2♡. You would raise to 4♡ with either of:

♠ A K 7 6 5	or	♠ A K 7 6
♡ A J 3 2		♡ A Q 3
◇ 4		◇ K 6 5
♣ Q 7 6		♣ Q 9 2

and the poor man is going to be completely in the dark as to whether you have a minimum opening with good heart support and distribution, like the first example, or a strong balanced hand with three hearts, like the second. How will he know whether to try for a slam or not?

Would it not be a better notion to bid the first hand:

| 1♠ | 2♡ |
| 4♡ | |

and the second:

1♠	2♡
2 NT (forcing)	anything
4♡	

Now partner knows what kind of raise to 4♡ he is facing, and can make his decision about slam with much more confidence.

There are other advantages to the forcing 2 NT rebid, and I am sure that you will discover them for yourselves if you adopt the treatment – one that I strongly recommend. Note, please, that the 2 NT rebid is forcing only after a two-level response to an opening bid. The auction:

> 1♡   1♠
> 2 NT

is still the old-fashioned 17–18 balanced.

Post Mortem (continued)

Pat had several lines of play open to her, and the decision to play on clubs after a couple of rounds of diamonds was certainly reasonable. It would have been better, as the cards actually lay, to play the first club from dummy, but there was no special reason to do this in the abstract. In general, if you have a suit like:

> A 10 9   Q 3 2

you should finesse twice through West, playing low to the 9, then later running the queen (or playing low to the 10) if East takes the jack on the first round. This is a better chance than running the 9 through East and later the queen through West, for the rule is: *Two missing honours are more likely to be split between the opponents than both held by one opponent.* This means that if you start by playing West for the jack but discover that East has it, West is more likely than East to have the king and you should arrange to play him for that card. You may like to consider why this is so, or you may simply take it on trust – there is a great chunk of mathematics coming up later in the book, and I do not propose to inflict another one on you at this stage.

Deal 6

East and West rapidly removed their cards from the board for the second deal of the round, and Pat remembered guiltily that they were supposed to be making up for lost time. 'Sorry,' she said, 'we need to be a little quicker, don't we?'

'You take your time,' said East kindly. 'Don't let the police worry you.'

'The police?' thought Chris, unaware that this was an often-used term among experienced players to refer to the Tournament Directors. There was no time to pursue the matter, though, for he was already the only player not to have taken out his cards for the next deal. When he did so, they looked like this:

Game All. Dealer North.

♠ Q J
♡ A J 10 9 4 3 2
♢ K 5 4
♣ Q

Pat and East passed, and Chris toyed with the idea of opening four hearts. This did not seem like the type of hand for such an adventure, though – the doubleton queen–jack of spades and the singleton queen of clubs might well be useful cards in defence but worthless in the play of the hand, which argued strongly against pre-emptive bidding. He settled for one heart, which appeared to give West something of a problem.

Finally, West emerged with a double and Pat considered her cards:

♠ A 9 5 4
♡ Q 8 7
◇ 8 3 2
♣ J 7 6

'I was about to bid one spade,' thought Pat, 'but would that be the most helpful thing to do now? It's likely that West has spades for his double, so the chances are that we don't belong in that suit. Perhaps I should bid one no trump – about right on values, but it doesn't tell Chris about my heart support, which could be very useful to him. Maybe two hearts is best, but this is such a flat hand. I could always pass, but that might shut us out of the auction altogether.'

What action would you take on Pat's hand?

Eventually, Pat decided to bid two hearts, with the idea of preventing East from bidding a minor suit at the two level, which might make it easier for the opponents to compete. East passed and Chris looked at his cards again. To pass would be feeble, he thought. Even though a raise to two hearts over a takeout double did not promise great strength, he was surely worth another effort. The question was: should he simply bid four hearts, or would it be better to make a trial bid of some kind?

Decide what action you would take before reading on.

'Well,' thought Chris, 'I nearly opened four hearts. Now that Pat has some support for me, I'm going to bid game.'

Everybody passed, and West led the ace of clubs. Chris contemplated the task of making ten tricks without much enthusiasm:

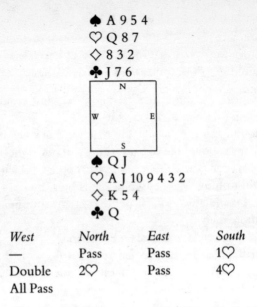

♠ A 9 5 4
♡ Q 8 7
♢ 8 3 2
♣ J 7 6

♠ Q J
♡ A J 10 9 4 3 2
♢ K 5 4
♣ Q

West	North	East	South
—	Pass	Pass	1♡
Double	2♡	Pass	4♡
All Pass			

East played the two on West's ace of clubs, Chris played the queen and West went into an interminable trance. Finally, to Chris's considerable surprise, West placed the king of clubs on the table at the second trick. How would you play the hand from this point?

Chris had assumed initially that West had the king of spades, the ace-king of clubs and the ace of diamonds for this double. That left room for East to hold the king of hearts, but meant that there were almost certainly four losers – three diamonds and a club. Now the picture had changed, for dummy's jack of clubs had become established for a diamond discard.

The implications of West's defence were not lost on Chris, however. West must have suspected that the king of clubs was going to be ruffed. If so, why had he led it? Surely a diamond switch would look far safer to West unless he had the ace, and even more surely a heart or a spade switch would look safer unless West had the kings of both suits. It was barely possible

66

that West was void in hearts, of course, but on the whole Chris was inclined to place West with every relevant high card.

The main hope was that West's king of hearts was singleton. What could be done otherwise? After considerable thought, Chris came up with a plan. This was the full deal:

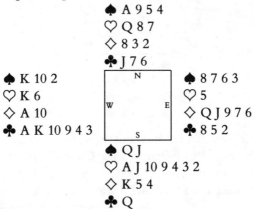

After ruffing the king of clubs, Chris led the queen of spades which West covered with the king and dummy won with the ace. The jack of clubs was cashed, and Chris discarded a diamond. Now a heart to the ace was followed by the jack of spades and a heart to West's king, leaving West on lead in this position:

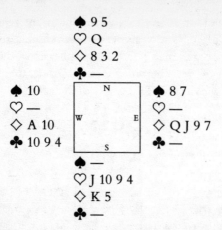

```
              ♠ 9 5
              ♡ Q
              ◇ 8 3 2
              ♣ —
  ♠ 10          N         ♠ 8 7
  ♡ —                     ♡ —
  ◇ A 10   W       E      ◇ Q J 9 7
  ♣ 10 9 4       S        ♣ —
              ♠ —
              ♡ J 10 9 4
              ◇ K 5
              ♣ —
```

Whatever West did, he could not defeat the contract – a club exit would be ruffed in dummy while Chris discarded his second diamond loser; the ten of spades would be ruffed, establishing dummy's nine for a diamond discard; the ace of diamonds was obviously futile. West gave the matter what appeared to be his usual lengthy consideration before trying the ace of diamonds in the forlorn hope that East had the king, and Chris claimed the rest feeling justifiably pleased with himself.

'Better if you play ace and another diamond after the ace of clubs holds, isn't it?' queried East.

'I don't think so,' said West after more thought. 'Declarer can cash two spades and play ace and another heart. I have to set up one of dummy's black suit cards then.'

Christ expected a word of praise from his partner, but Pat was hurriedly scribbling the score on the travelling score slip and putting it back in the board. She completed this task just as the familiar tones of the director asked the players to move for the next round, and she looked up at the official in triumph.

Chris's decision not to open four hearts was very sound. The heart suit was not quite good enough in the first place, but more significant was the presence of the minor honours in the black suits. Frequently, pre-emptive openings do not achieve the desired result because unsupported queens and jacks add nothing to the playing strength of the hand, but combine to ensure that the opponents can make very little. Compare these two pairs of hands:

(1) ♠ J 3 2 ♠ 10 4
   ♡ 8 4 ♡ A K Q J 10 9 7
   ◇ A 10 3 2 ◇ 9 4
   ♣ J 9 6 5 ♣ 8 2

(2) ♠ J 3 2 ♠ Q 4
   ♡ 8 4 ♡ A K Q J 10 9 7
   ◇ A 10 3 2 ◇ J 9
   ♣ J 9 6 5 ♣ Q 2

The West hand is the same in each case. Consider what might happen if East opens four hearts at game all on hand (1), and this is doubled and passed out. East will take eight tricks and concede 500 points, but this is no tragedy, for the opponents can surely make four spades and possibly five spades for 620 or 650. If East opens four hearts on hand (2), though – which is apparently a stronger hand – he will concede the same 500 points if doubled, and this time he will regret it, for his side is very likely to have at least four and possibly five tricks to take against a spade contract by the enemy. Even if four hearts is not doubled on hand (2), minus 200 is likely to represent a very poor score.

When considering whether to open a marginal pre-empt, then, you should be less inclined to do so if your hand contains a holding such as Q 5, Q 6 4, J 5 or J 6 4.

Returning to the actual deal, West's double of one heart is the normal move on a hand too strong for a simple overcall. He was hoping that the auction would allow him to bid his clubs on the next round, conveying the message of a good hand with a good club suit.

Pat's decision over the takeout double is an awkward one. Many players have the agreement that they will simply 'ignore the double', bidding what they would have bid anyway – in this case, one spade. That has the merit of simplicity, but may not be the best approach in every case. When the opponents make a takeout double, it is often important for you to show support for your partner's suit immediately if you have it, for the enemy are in the auction and may make it very awkward for you to show support later. Moreover, the act of raising partner's suit takes away bidding room from the opponents, which may hinder their search for their best fit.

Chris's decision to simply bid four hearts was a trifle rash. A more cautious player might have contented himself with a trial bid. The question then arises: what trial bid would be appropriate?

Long suit trial bids

A very common position in bridge is this: you and your partner have bid and supported a suit, and you feel that if the hands fit well you have a good chance of game, while if they fit poorly you would be wise to stay out . How can you investigate this fit?

Frequently, the degree of fit will depend on whether your own losers are facing losers in partner's hand, or whether partner can take care of your side-suit losers while you can take care of hers. Consider these two pairs of hands:

(1) ♠ Q J 3 2   ♠ A K 10 9 5
  ♥ 6   ♥ 7 3 2
  ♦ K 9 4 2   ♦ A 5
  ♣ 9 8 6 4   ♣ K Q 7

(2) ♠ Q J 3 2   ♠ A K 10 9 5
  ♥ 6   ♥ K Q 7
  ♦ K 9 4 2   ♦ A 5
  ♣ 9 8 6 4   ♣ 7 3 2

In both cases, the auction starts with one spade by East and two spades by West. On hand (1), if East simply bids four spades he will make it, perhaps with an overtrick, unless he is very unlucky. On hand (2) four spades has almost no chance at all. Yet the West hands are identical, and the East hands have simply had two suits exchanged – hearts and clubs.

You can see that the factor which determines the success or failure of the game contract is West's ability to take care of losers in the suit where East has three small. What East needs to be able to do is to indicate to West that this is the case.

For this reason, many players adopt what are called 'long suit trial bids' (see page three onwards). After one spade – two spades, East bids a suit where he has losers. West bids three spades or four spades depending on her ability to take care of those losers. On the two pairs of hands above, the auctions would be:

(1) West	East	(2) West	East
—	1♠	—	1♠
2♠	3♥	2♠	3♣
4♠	Pass	3♠	Pass

Many variations and refinements of this treatment are possible, but the basic idea is simple enough and will make bidding games on marginal values less of a hit–or–miss affair.

Post Mortem (continued)

Chris might have issued a long suit game try with three diamonds – the suit in which he had a number of potential losers – and this would have been firmly rejected by Pat. As it was, Chris found himself, not for the first time, in a contract where his prospects were somewhat dismal.

When West unexpectedly led the king of clubs, Chris did well to consider why his opponent was apparently being so friendly. It may have been, of course, that West had simply made a mistake, but Chris had formed the impression that this West was unlikely to do anything risky or silly without good reason. It is always a good idea to place yourself mentally in your opponent's position when he does something unexpected, and to ask yourself: 'Now, why would I do that if I were in this position?'

Having thought it through, Chris played with great skill to give himself the best chance. There was nothing that West could do to prevent the end position which arose, but Chris had to see the possibilities that the nine of spades presented.

The score
Plus 620 was a very fine result for North–South, matched by only one other pair. Chris smugly wrote down nine out of ten for his estimate, feeling that he was being a little conservative.

He would have felt a trifle less self-satisfied, perhaps, had he examined the score sheet with greater attention. At most tables, the contract was a more modest three hearts, and every declarer had scored exactly nine tricks for plus 140. Had Chris played the hand in three hearts as he in fact played in four, he would have scored plus 170.

It is an often-ignored feature of pairs scoring that plus 170 beats plus 140 by just as much as plus 620 does – that is, two match points. Minus 100, though, loses to plus 140 by the same amount. What this means it that at pairs, unlike any other form

72

of scoring, there is no real need to press for close game contracts.

It often happens that an expert partnership does not perform as well in a pairs game as their form undoubtedly suggests. One of the reasons for this is that an expert will bid what he knows to be a close game on the grounds that his superior card play will give him an extra chance of making it. So it might – but he is still wrong to bid it.

Let us examine what happens to an expert who bids a game that nobody else contemplates. On a good day, he will play brilliantly to make it for 620 and a top, since the field will be scoring 140 in their part score. On a bad day, even the expert's brilliance will be unequal to the task of making game, and he will score minus 100 for a bottom.

Now suppose that our expert refrains from bidding game. On a good day, he scores plus 170 – but this is still a top, for the field is still scoring plus 140. On a bad day, he scores 140 like the rest of the field – but this time, he scores an average. However good you are, if you risk half the match points on every board on the chance that your superior skill will be rewarded, you are not making the best use of that skill – in fact, you are throwing most of it away.

Deal 7

'Going a little better after that first round,' said Pat cheerfully.

'Yes,' said Chris, 'but I don't think it's going to get any easier.'

Wondering what her partner meant, Pat looked idly at the convention card which their opponents for the next two deals had placed on the table. The light dawned when she saw the two names at the top, and realized that they were due to play the round against one of the country's foremost international pairs.

'When I played my clubs in the order 6–8–3,' one of them was saying, 'surely it was obvious that I didn't want you to switch to a heart unless you had the king. Declarer would never have taken the spade hook with 2–4–1–6, and you knew from the diamond cue that you couldn't afford to break the minors. Anyone with half a brain would have . . .'

He seemed disposed to continue in this vein for some hours, but Pat decided that if they were to have any chance of starting the round, let alone finishing it, in the allotted fifteen minutes, she was going to have to take the initiative.

'Good afternoon,' she said politely.

The effect was twofold. West, the grumbler, looked startled but subsided into a semi-audible mumble in which the word 'cretin' could ocasionally be distinguished. East, however, returned Pat's greeting with considerable warmth and a smile of what looked very like relief.

Chris took his cards from the board, wondering vaguely why experts used different implements from everybody else to play bridge. What was a spade hook, and a diamond cue? Whose telephone number was 683 2416? Still, he thought, West was right about not being able to afford to break the miners. Look what happened to Edward Heath.

This was deal 23:

Game All.
Dealer East

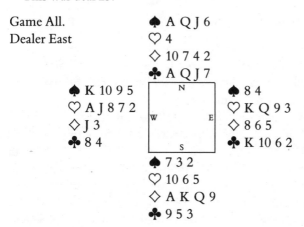

♠ A Q J 6
♡ 4
♢ 10 7 4 2
♣ A Q J 7

♠ K 10 9 5
♡ A J 8 7 2
♢ J 3
♣ 8 4

♠ 8 4
♡ K Q 9 3
♢ 8 6 5
♣ K 10 6 2

♠ 7 3 2
♡ 10 6 5
♢ A K Q 9
♣ 9 5 3

'Pass,' said East.

Weren't you supposed to say 'No bid'? thought Chris. Perhaps that was only for players below international status. Not to be outdone, he also volunteered 'Pass', bringing a grin from his partner.

'One heart,' said West.

'Double,' said Pat firmly.

'Stop, please,' said East. 'Three hearts.'

West struck the table a sharp blow, and Chris looked at him enquiringly. 'That is a pre-emptive bid,' explained West. 'He should have good heart support, but will have less than the normal strength for a raise to three hearts.'

'Thank you,' said Chris. 'No bid.'

Pat couldn't resist it. 'Don't you mean Pass?' she enquired innocently, and even West managed a faint smile.

When order had been restored, West passed and Pat, though

feeling that somehow her side was being talked out of something, could not bring herself to make a further positive call. The auction had been:

West	North	East	South
		Pass	Pass
1♡	Double	3♡	All Pass

Pat considered her opening lead only briefly. A black suit, away from the A Q J, was surely too dangerous, and a trump might easily ruin her partner's holding. She led the two of diamonds, and East put down his dummy.

'Thank you, partner,' said West. 'Small, please.'

Chris, grateful that his partner seemed to have found a good lead, swiftly cashed the queen and king of diamonds. Without really pausing for thought, he followed with the ace which was ruffed by West. Playing at the same rapid tempo, West drew three rounds of trumps with the king, queen and ace. Pat followed to the first of these, discarded her remaining diamond on the second, then threw her small club on the third.

Ever since the second round of diamonds, Pat had been feeling pleased with herself. Surely, she was going to take at least two spade tricks and the ace of clubs, and international player or not, West was going down in his contract. Pride, though, goeth before destruction, and when at the sixth trick declarer led the five of spades from his hand, Pat saw no reason to 'waste' one of her honours and followed with the six.

'Eight, please,' said declarer, and Chris looked a trifle bemused as he followed with the two.

Horrified, Pat began feverishly to wonder how she was going to explain this lapse of concentration. After a moment, though, she reflected that since declarer still had three spades left and could ruff only one of them in the dummy, perhaps she would still come to her two spade tricks and all would be well. This was the position:

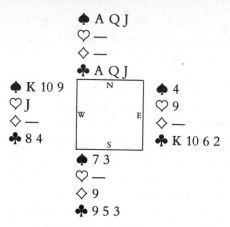

A spade was led from dummy, and Pat won with the jack over West's nine. Clinging to the notion that her spade tenace must be protected at all costs, she tried a desperate queen of clubs. West sat upright in his chair, called for the king of clubs which held the trick, and played a second club from dummy. This left:

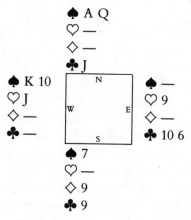

and Pat, on lead, could see only too clearly that a spade would allow declarer's king to score a trick, while a club would establish dummy's ten.

'I'm terribly sorry, Chris,' she said. 'Playing low on that spade was really stupid. We had him one down easily.'

'I am not sure that even that would have been especially good for you,' said East gently.

Still trembling, Pat opened the travelling score slip. At most tables, North–South had played the hand in a part score in diamonds, making nine or ten tricks for scores of 110 or 130. At only a few others, East–West had been defeated by one trick in three hearts for 100 to North–South, so as East had envisaged, Pat's calamitous defence had cost only a handful of match points. Even so, the indignity of having to enter minus 140 for a complete bottom was painful. Inwardly vowing revenge, Pat placed the next board on the table.

Post Mortem

It is, of course, inexcusably rude to arrive at a new table in the middle of an argument (or in West's case a monologue) with your partner. It is also unfair, for it reduces the amount of playing time available to you *and* your opponents. Should any-one behave like this, you are fully entitled to shut them up – but there is no need to be abrupt yourself, for a pointed 'Good afternoon' is perfectly effective.

Bridge has a wealth of jargon, some of which is incomprehensible to inexperienced players. Experts use it all the time, chiefly because it is a convenient shorthand for discussion, but occasionally purely for effect. Try not to be intimidated, and treat the delicate ego of the expert with what indulgence you can find.

For reference, a 'hook' is an American term for a finesse, and a 'diamond cue' is short for a cue-bid in diamonds. '2–4–1–6' refers to a hand with two spades, four hearts, one diamond and six clubs. 'Breaking' a suit means being the first player to lead it. Now you know.

In Britain, it is usual to say 'No bid', but 'Pass' is perfectly acceptable. You should stick to one or the other, though.

In the auction, West's opening bid was appreciably short of the normal values. Such gambits are common at all forms of bridge, but particularly at pairs, when it is no disaster to overbid and go down if you have talked the opponents out of a more profitable contract of their own. If partner has already passed, a light opening bid carries little risk that partner will have a really strong hand and carry the auction too high, so openings of this nature are especially favoured when third to speak. There are still dangers in such tactics, of course, and you will form your own opinion of their effectiveness.

Pat's double of one heart was quite correct, with an opening bid and good support for whatever suit her partner might be forced to select.

East chose well in selecting three hearts. The reasoning behind the use of this bid as a pre-emptive measure is this: if our side has a good fit in one of the suits (hearts), it is practically certain that oppponents also have a fit in another suit. By raising the level of the auction as high as possible quickly, we make it much harder for opponents to locate their fit at a safe level. If partner has a good hand, he can still carry on to game.

Raising partner following a take-out double

If three hearts is pre-emptive, what should East do with a genuine raise to three hearts? – say:

♠ 8 4
♡ K 10 9 3
♢ A 6 5
♣ K 10 6 2

The obvious solution of bidding three hearts loudly is frowned upon by the law-makers. The answer is to use a conventional bid to replace the 'lost' natural bid of three hearts, and the bid chosen is two no-trumps. So in the auction:

West	North	East	South
1♡	Double	?	

you bid 3♡ (pre-emptive) with:

> ♠ 8 4
> ♡ K Q 9 3
> ◇ 8 6 5
> ♣ K 10 6 2

and 2 NT (a real raise to three hearts) with:

> ♠ 8 4
> ♡ K 10 9 3
> ◇ A 6 5
> ♣ K 10 6 2

If you have stayed with me so far, you will want to know what you do with a real bid of two no-trumps – say:

> ♠ A 10 3
> ♡ 8 6
> ◇ K J 9 7
> ♣ K 10 6 2

The answer is to redouble. This call usually shows a strongish hand with shortage in hearts, which hopes to double the opponents for penalties in the later stages. But it can also be used as the first move on a hand such as the one above, where you intend to complete the description with a later bid of 2 NT – though you could consider a double of 2♣ or 2◇ should the enemy select either contract.

Post Mortem (continued)

Over three hearts, Chris had to decide whether or not to bid four diamonds. His partner had promised, in principle, support for diamonds and was likely to have one heart or none. Three small spades and three small clubs did not look promising, though, and it is easy to sympathize with his actual pass. If you would have bid four diamonds, your play would have to be as accurate as your bidding is bold to emerge with ten tricks and a plus score.

West had clearly done more than enough on his hand, and Pat had the final decision for her side. Suppose that you had decided to bid with her hand, what call would you have made?

The second take-out double

It is vital to remember that if a player doubles a suit for take-out, when she doubles the same suit again, that has *not* suddenly become a penalty double. It is still for take-out, simply showing a better than minimum hand and continuing to request co-operation from partner. So, if you have:

♠ A Q J 4
♡ 7
♢ A Q J 5
♣ K Q 6 2

and the bidding proceeds:

West	North	East	South
1♡	Double	2♡	Pass
Pass	?		

you should double again – still for take-out, still asking partner to bid his best suit.

Moving to the other side of the table, if you have:

♠ 6 5 3 2
♡ 10 6 3
♢ 7 6 2
♣ 8 7 5

after the bidding:

West	North	East	South
1♡	Double	2♡	Pass
Pass	Double	Pass	?

do *not* pass! Partner does not want you to pass – she wants your best suit. It is not much of a suit, true, but you have four of them and you can at least bid them at the two level.

'I had to pass, partner – I had nothing in my hand!'

'So I see – and nothing between your ears, either.'

Post Mortem (continued)

I hope you will agree, having studied the above, that if you would bid over three hearts on Pat's hand, you would use a second take-out double. Again, full marks for courage.

At any rate, three hearts became the final contract. The diamond lead was certainly not wrong, and the play proceeded normally until the fateful sixth trick.

We will draw a veil over Pat's play of a low spade when declarer led one towards the eight. She was a little caught up in the rapid tempo of the play – it could happen to anyone.

Of far more concern is Pat's play at trick nine. This, you remember, the position with the defence needing two tricks:

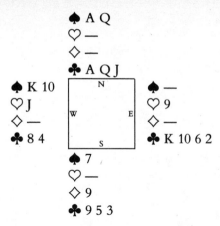

```
              ♠ A Q
              ♡ —
              ◇ —
              ♣ A Q J
  ♠ K 10      ┌─────────┐      ♠ —
  ♡ J         │    N    │      ♡ 9
  ◇ —         │ W     E │      ◇ —
  ♣ 8 4       │    S    │      ♣ K 10 6 2
              └─────────┘
              ♠ 7
              ♡ —
              ◇ 9
              ♣ 9 5 3
```

and *North knew it*. Having already given up a spade trick, though, Pat was determined not to give up another one. Of course, playing the ace of spades would allow declarer to ruff in dummy and establish his king. But it would also place the lead in dummy, who would have to lead a club away from the king to give North two club tricks!

Pat's actual play of a club was, as we have seen, doomed to failure. It happens often that the first mistake, or wrong guess, that you make is not actually fatal. It becomes fatal only because in brooding on it, you fall victim to panic and despair. You concentrate on one suit to the exclusion of the whole hand. You lose track, you lose count, you lose confidence. Above all, you lose concentration – the single most powerful attribute of the winning player.

How can you recover? The best way is simply – take your time. Try even harder to reconstruct the unseen hands, and to consider even more carefully the effect of each play you might make. Don't, as so many players will, play any old card out of self-disgust and a desire to end the nightmare. Just pick yourself up, dust yourself down . . .

The score

Minus 140 was a complete zero for Pat and Chris, a severe blow to their chances. They would need somehow to score well on the next deal, a tall order against this particular pair.

Deal 8

Pat picked up her cards for the next deal, and was confronted with a hand containing no high card points, but an exciting distribution:

♠10 8 6 5 4
♡10 8 7 5 3 2
♢ 6
♣ 5

She was just about to pass when it occurred to her that here was the chance to obtain her revenge for the last board. East and West sat impassively, examining their cards and exuding confidence. Chris, who to his credit had said nothing about the awful result on the previous deal, was studying his hand anxiously. Well, she would show these internationals that she was not a player to be trifled with! For the first time in her young life, Pat deliberately opened with a psychic bid – a bluff, designed to fool the opponents into believing she had strength.

'One heart,' said Pat.

'Pass,' said East, unconcerned. Chris went into a deep study, and Pat began to feel decidedly uneasy. When you make a psychic bid, you are hoping that the opponents will be deceived by your show of strength into underestimating their combined resources. The risk, of course, is that if your partner has a good hand, he will take the auction far too high on the basis of your bid. It appeared that East had nothing, but Chris clearly had some good cards. It seemed like an age before he spoke.

'Two clubs,' he said. West passed, looking slightly bored, and Pat contemplated a new problem. If she passed, it would reveal her bluff to the whole table, and surely East and West were good enough players to know what to do. 'I've started,' she thought to herself, 'so I'll finish. If ♡10 8 7 5 3 2 was good enough to open, then ♠10 8 6 5 4 ought to be good enough for a reverse.'

'Two spades,' said Pat, By this time, of course, her initial act of daring had gone to her head a little – two hearts might have been a safer bid. East passed, and Chris had his next bid ready in far less time than his first had taken.

'Stop, please,' he said to West with a courtesy that was ever so slightly exaggerated. 'Four no-trumps.'

West scrupulously considered his hand for a measured ten seconds. During this time, Pat had gone into a complete panic – but not so complete that she failed to alert for Chris's conventional Blackwood call. West nodded gravely to acknowledge the alert, then passed.

Pat's thoughts, as you may imagine, were in total disarray. Her first impulse was simply to pass, but four no-trumps was not likely to be a good contract. Perhaps she should just respond to Blackwood with five clubs to show no aces. But she had opened the bidding and then reversed, so surely Chris would not expect no aces and – horrible thought – might believe she had four! The prospect of playing in a grand slam with no aces in the combined hands so appalled her that, without further thought, she simply bid the contract that she wanted to play in. Perhaps by some miracle Chris would pass, and it might not be too bad. If not . . . well, maybe Chris would have forgiven her in a year or so, and they could try to qualify again next year.

'Five hearts,' said Pat. Chris alerted, but East passed without enquiry. Chris, with a disappointed shrug, bid six no-trumps.

West passed, Pat did likewise, but East seemed slightly mystified. He turned to Chris and said:

'One heart and two spades were natural, were they?'

'Yes,' said Chris, 'just basic Acol.'

'Four no–trumps simple Blackwood?' pursued East.

'Yes,' replied Chris, 'and five hearts showed two aces.'

'Thank, you,' said East. 'Double.'

As if in a nightmare, Pat heard her partner redouble confidently. West passed, and Pat considered wildly whether she should run to seven hearts. What about running to seven spades? What about running upstairs to bed and not coming out for a week? Finally, she passed and prepared to take her medicine. At least afterwards she could take Chris to the bar for a double brandy. Or possibly, in the circumstances, a redoubled brandy.

West led a heart, and Pat put down the dummy. She braced herself for her partner's wrath, but Chris's good temper still held firm. He gulped, took three deep breaths, and then did one of the hardest things he had ever done at the bridge table.

'Thank you, partner,' he said.

This was the full hand:

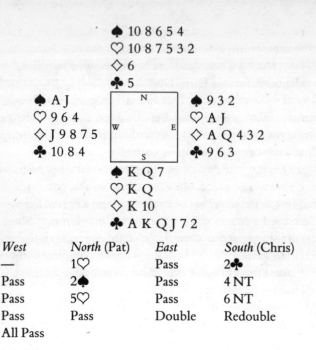

	♠ 10 8 6 5 4		
	♡ 10 8 7 5 3 2		
	◇ 6		
	♣ 5		

♠ A J   N   ♠ 9 3 2
♡ 9 6 4   ♡ A J
◇ J 9 8 7 5   W   E   ◇ A Q 4 3 2
♣ 10 8 4   S   ♣ 9 6 3

	♠ K Q 7		
	♡ K Q		
	◇ K 10		
	♣ A K Q J 7 2		

West	North (Pat)	East	South (Chris)
—	1♡	Pass	2♣
Pass	2♠	Pass	4 NT
Pass	5♡	Pass	6 NT
Pass	Pass	Double	Redouble
All Pass			

While Pat had been laying down her dummy, East had been
having trouble with his spectacles. He had taken out his handkerchief and was polishing one of the lenses with an irritated air.
Chris called for a small heart. East put down his glasses and
handkerchief, picked up his cards, and drew out the ace of
diamonds, which he played.

West stiffened imperceptibly, and seemed to be biting his
tongue. Chris, trying not to look too mystified, won the heart
trick with the queen and was about to lead to the next trick.
Before he could do so, East had led the ace of hearts.

'I think,' murmured West, 'that we had better have the director over before this goes any further.'

'I agree with you,' said Chris. 'Director, please!'

'What is all the fuss about?' enquired East.

'If you were to put your glasses back on and look at the card

88

you have just led,' suggested West with dangerous mildness, 'you would see – in both senses.'

East replaced his spectacles, contemplated the ace of hearts for a couple of seconds, then dissolved into helpless laughter. Pat, relieved by the thought that perhaps the board would have to be cancelled and they would be awarded an average, started laughing too, and by the time the Director arrived, he found the entire table too hysterical to speak for a while.

Finally, everyone calmed down and the facts were explained. The Director cogitated briefly, then consulted the rule book which he carried with him before addressing the table.

'The ace of diamonds is a played card to the first trick,' he said, 'and that trick stands as played and belongs to declarer. The ace of diamonds is also, of course, a revoke, and because East has led to the next trick, albeit out of turn, it is an established revoke. Do you understand so far?'

Everybody nodded. 'The offending player did not win the revoke trick,' continued the Director, 'so the penalty for the revoke will be one trick, plus another trick if East wins a trick with a card he could legally have played to the first trick. Assuming,' he added, 'that the offending side wins any tricks at all.'

'At the rate we're going,' said West under his breath, 'that seems a very remote possibility.'

The director paused to see whether the players were following his explanation. East and West, he knew, were totally familiar with the Laws, but Pat and Chris were newcomers and had to be told their rights clearly. Pat was not really concentrating – she was worried that the hand was going to have to be played out after all, and though the defenders appeared to have to transfer some tricks to Chris, she seriously doubted whether that would be enough. Chris, though, thought briefly about what the Director had said, then indicated that he understood.

'The ace of hearts,' said the Director to Chris, 'is a lead out of turn, since East did not win the first trick. You therefore have the following options: first, you may accept the lead. Do you wish to exercise this option?'

'No,' said Chris.

'Correct,' said West, and there was more laughter.

'The ace of hearts is now a major penalty card,' said the Director. 'It remains face up on the table in front of East. East must play it at his first legal opportunity. Should West obtain the lead before East has played the ace of hearts, you may require West to lead a heart or forbid West from doing so. If you exercise either of those options, East may pick up the ace of hearts – it will no longer be a penalty card. Otherwise, the card remains a penalty card, but West may lead whatever he wishes. Do you understand your options?'

'I think so,' said Chris, 'but don't go too far away, will you please?'

'I may as well stay to watch the play,' said the Director. 'It looks as though it'll be a good story to tell the other Directors over dinner.'

This was now the position, with South on lead having, remarkably, lost no tricks:

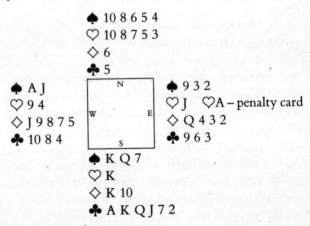

```
                    ♠ 10 8 6 5 4
                    ♡ 10 8 7 5 3
                    ◇ 6
                    ♣ 5
      ♠ A J                              ♠ 9 3 2
      ♡ 9 4                              ♡ J   ♡ A – penalty card
      ◇ J 9 8 7 5                        ◇ Q 4 3 2
      ♣ 10 8 4                           ♣ 9 6 3
                    ♠ K Q 7
                    ♡ K
                    ◇ K 10
                    ♣ A K Q J 7 2
```

Chris cashed six rounds of clubs, on the fourth of which East had to discard the ace of hearts. The king of hearts now dropped East's jack, and Chris played the king of spades. West won with the ace and returned a diamond, but Chris won with the king and cashed the queen of spades. When this dropped West's jack, Chris was able to cross the dummy's ten of spades to discard his losing diamond on the ten of hearts.

'Right,' said the Director. 'The offending side won one trick after the revoke, so that must be transferred to you. Thus the result should be scored as six-no-trumps redoubled, made with an overtrick, which comes to . . . er . . .'

'1860,' said East.

'That was quick!' said Pat admiringly. 'How do you know those scores so fast?'

'It's practice,' said East sadly.

Post Mortem

The use of 'psychic', or bluff bids is always a controversial topic. There are those who hold that such bids are tantamount to cheating – 'We play bridge', they will tell you, 'not poker'. Others will reply that deception is a vital part of the game, which adds greatly to its fascination, and psychic bidding is simply another deceptive tactic.

Law 40 of the game is quite clear: *'A player may make any call or play (including an intentionally misleading call – such as a psychic bid . . .) without prior announcement, provided that such call or play is not based on a partnership understanding.'* This means that provided you have no prior understanding with your partner that you will – or are likely to – use psychic bids in a particular situation, you are free to perpetrate the most outrageous bluffs.

Those who like to chance their arm in this way will often attempt to justify their actions by the argument that: 'I have two opponents who may be deceived, and only one partner, so the odds are clearly in my favour!' This is a fallacy, of course – the opponents, unlike your partner, are under no obligation to trust you. When you attempt a bluff, what you are really hoping is that although your partner will be deceived, this will not matter as much as the fact that your opponents are also fooled.

Most experienced players – even, if the truth be known, those who indulge in the tactic of the out-and-out psychic from time to time – will tell you that the success rate of such bids is fairly low. They are what is known as 'top-or-bottom' actions – they will result in an abnormal score which is sometimes a top but far more frequently a bottom. They are a desperate remedy for a desperate situation, but when they succeed, they can be a source of great satisfaction.

On this particular deal, of course, Pat's psychic should have worked calamitously. Consider how you think the North–South cards would normally be bid before reading further.

A good auction on the North–South cards might be:

North	South	North	South
♠ 10 8 6 5 4	♠ K Q 7	Pass	2 ♣
♡ 10 8 7 5 3 2	♡ K Q	2 ♢	2 NT
♢ 6	♢ K 10	3 ♢	3 ♡
♣ 5	♣ A K Q J 7 2	3 ♠	3 NT
		4 ♡	4 ♠
		Pass	

On hearing a negative response to the strong 2♣ opening, South abandons thoughts of a slam and concentrates on the most likely game. Thus 2 NT is a better rebid than 3♣ – if partner passes, you will be in reasonable contract; if not, you will probably end up in 3 NT but you should give your side a chance at a major suit fit. 3♢ is a transfer, showing hearts, and the rest of the auction is natural.

Four spades is no bargain, of course, and might be defeated by good defence even with the fortunate position of the cards. Still, four spades or four hearts are normal contracts. The same cannot really be said of six no-trumps redoubled, which was the result of Pat's outlandish opening bid and her subsequent panic-stricken actions.

Even the finest of players are not immune from the occasional mechanical error. The great Belladonna once lost an international tournament because of a revoke. This does not, however, mean that the next time you arrive in six no-trumps redoubled missing three aces against two internationals, you are going to make an overtrick. Perhaps a higher power decided that Chris deserved to be rewarded for keeping his vow not to shout at his partner.

The legal complexities that resulted from East's spectacular defence (or unspectacular, since he had his glasses off at the time) were handled very well by the Director. It is the duty of that official to make sure that he has explained to the players all their options and the consequences of each one. This includes the option to condone an irregularity, such as accepting a lead out of turn. Too often, players are not given this option when they are entitled to it.

The score
Plus 1860 was, it will not surprise you to learn, a top for Chris and Pat. This brought their score on the round back up to average, and kept them more or less on course.

Deal 9

'Excuse me,' said a voice from behind Pat's chair. 'Would you mind sitting forward a little?'

Pat complied automatically, but wondered why anyone should have a problem getting through the gap between her chair and that of South at the next table. The question resolved itself when on the corner of the table by her left hand were placed: a pint of beer, a plate containing three rounds of sandwiches, a packet of crisps and a Mars bar. These items were followed after an interval by the appearance of East, who took his seat gingerly at first as if to satisfy himself that the sturdy hotel chair would not collapse under his colossal bulk.

'Hello,' said this individual jovially. 'Partner will be along in a minute. He's just gone to the bar.'

When West arrived a few seconds later, Pat had to bite her lip to stop herself from giggling, for a greater contrast to the gentleman overflowing the East chair could scarcely be imagined. The tiny, birdlike figure took his seat, sipped fastidiously from his glass of diet tonic water and poured a handful of peanuts into the palm of his hand, whence he pecked at them at regular intervals.

'Fatman and Robin,' thought Pat to herself, and blew her nose to cover her suppressed laughter.

She picked up her cards for the ninth deal:

Game All. Dealer South.

♠ K 3 2
♡ 3
♢ A J 9 6
♣ A J 9 6 2

Chris passed as dealer, and rather to Pat's surprise, West opened one club. Pat passed, East bid one heart and West rebid two clubs.

Pat's hopes of defending against this contract were dashed when East bid two diamonds. West, after another sip of tonic, bid three hearts and East carried on to four hearts.

Pat considered briefly whether she ought to double. After all, she knew that clubs would not provide many tricks for the opponents, she seemed to have a good holding in diamonds, and perhaps the trumps would break badly. But the opponents had bid strongly – East had not limited his hand at all – so Pat concluded that double would be too great a risk.

Chris led the five of diamonds against four hearts, and West put down the dummy:

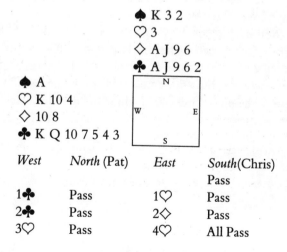

♠ K 3 2
♡ 3
♢ A J 9 6
♣ A J 9 6 2

♠ A
♡ K 10 4
♢ 10 8
♣ K Q 10 7 5 4 3

West	North (Pat)	East	South (Chris)
			Pass
1♣	Pass	1♡	Pass
2♣	Pass	2♢	Pass
3♡	Pass	4♡	All Pass

With the space of a couple of seconds, declarer drank a quarter of his pint of beer, ate one of his sandwiches, and said: 'Thank you, partner, very nice, small diamond please.' Pat won the trick with the ace, East playing the four, and paused to consider her defence. How would you plan to defend the contract?

'Prospects do not look great,' thought Pat. 'I wonder why Chris has led a diamond, not a spade? It can't be a singleton, for that would leave declarer with six, and it's not as if Chris could have a very dangerous spade holding. Still, never mind about that. It doesn't look as though declarer will be able to use the club suit, so he is going to have to ruff some of his losing spades and maybe his diamonds in the dummy. I'm going to switch to a trump – if that picks up an honour in Chris's hand, too bad.'

Pat led the three of hearts. Declarer played the two, Chris the five and dummy won the trick with the ten. The ace of spades was cashed, and declarer called for dummy's king of clubs. What should Pat do now?

Pat, of course, was ready for this. She had formed the strong impression that declarer rather than Chris was void in clubs. Of course, declarer could discard a loser on the king of clubs if she did not cover, but Pat had gauged that declarer would not risk this, for if the king of clubs ran to the ace and another trump was returned declarer would be poorly placed. Moreover, it was her experience that fat men who drank beer never believed that a woman would calmly duck an ace when a king was led from the dummy. She played the two of clubs and declarer, pausing only to eat another sandwich, ruffed. This had been the full deal:

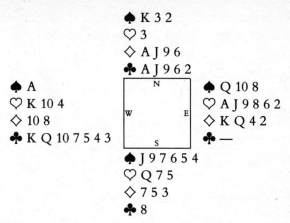

♠ K 3 2
♡ 3
♢ A J 9 6
♣ A J 9 6 2

♠ A
♡ K 10 4
♢ 10 8
♣ K Q 10 7 5 4 3

♠ Q 10 8
♡ A J 9 8 6 2
♢ K Q 4 2
♣ —

♠ J 9 7 6 5 4
♡ Q 7 5
♢ 7 5 3
♣ 8

and the position was now:

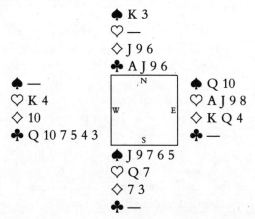

♠ K 3
♡ —
♢ J 9 6
♣ A J 9 6

♠ —
♡ K 4
♢ 10
♣ Q 10 7 5 4 3

♠ Q 10
♡ A J 9 8
♢ K Q 4
♣ —

♠ J 9 7 6 5
♡ Q 7
♢ 7 3
♣ —

Declarer ruffed a spade in dummy and led another low club, which he ruffed with the eight of hearts. Chris overruffed with the queen and led another trump, leaving declarer with a losing spades and a losing diamond in his hand, and no trump on the table to cope with either. One down.

'Sorry, partner,' said East. 'Never thought this lady would duck the ace of clubs.' He drank another quarter of a pint. Pat smiled inwardly.

Post Mortem

At pairs scoring more than at other forms of the game, it is right to consider a double when you are aware that at least one suit and possibly more lies badly for the declarer. At teams or at rubber bridge, such doubles are risky since they may give away too much information, so that it is usually right to double only if you feel that two down or more is likely.

In general, however, this kind of double is worthwhile only if one of two conditions holds: (a) You have a strong holding in dummy's first bid suit and are keen that partner should lead it. This almost always applies only to contracts in no trumps; or (b) The opponents have both made limited bids during the auction, so that you are aware that the final contract has been bid on limited values.

In this case, Pat was certainly correct not to double, for East had not limited his hand at all and West had shown extra values in support of hearts. Had Pat doubled, declarer would have had little difficulty with the play of the hand.

Chris's opening lead was certainly bizarre. He explained afterwards that he really wanted to lead a trump, since that seemed strongly indicated on the bidding. His nerve failed him, however, and he could not bring himself to lead the five of hearts from three to the queen. The trouble was that having intended to lead one red suit five and decided against it, he had accidentally found himself leading the other one!

His actual choice worked very well in a strange way. Had he led a normal spade, declarer would have won the ace and called immediately for the king of clubs. Pat would have found it much harder to duck this smoothly, and if she had played the ace of clubs declarer would ruff, ruff a spade in dummy and lead a diamond, making ten tricks easily enough.

As the play went, Pat had time to consider her defence carefully after winning the ace of diamonds. Her trump switch was the logical move, but more important was the fact that she had time to prepare herself for the play of the king of clubs from dummy.

Anticipating a problem

How many times have you found yourself making tell-tale pauses during the play of a hand when declarer leads a card? The types of position in which a declarer can put the defenders to an unpleasant test are very numerous, such as this:

Dummy
♠ K J 3 2

You
♠ A 8 6 5

Hearts are trumps and declarer leads the ten of spades from his hand. Do you play low and risk declarer having a singleton, so that you never make your ace of spades which could be the decisive trick? Or do you duck, hoping that declarer will finesse against your presumed queen?

Or this:

Dummy
♠ A J 8 5

You
♠ Q 4 3

There are no trumps and declarer again leads the ten of spades from his hand. Do you cover, lest the position is:

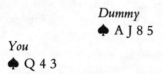

Or do you duck, in case the position is:

$$\spadesuit \text{ A J } 8\,5$$
$$\spadesuit \text{ Q } 4\,3 \qquad\qquad \spadesuit \text{ } 7\,6\,2$$
$$\spadesuit \text{ K } 10\,9$$

when declarer may misguess the suit if you do not cover?

There are, of course, no hard and fast rules, and even the greatest of players occasionally do the wrong thing when put to the test – especially if it occurs early in the hand.

However, your chances of doing the right thing are greatly improved if you fall into the habit of anticipating these problems before they occur. This means that when declarer leads the testing card, you will at least be ready with your play in tempo, and will not make an idiot pause which gives the whole show away. You may still play the wrong card, but as the great Scottish author Hugh Kelsey once wrote: 'Partners are far more likely to forgive a wrong card played smoothly than a giveaway pause.'

This means that when the dummy puts down a suit headed by the king-jack, and you have the ace sitting under dummy, you should mentally decide there and then what you are going to do when declarer leads the suit from his hand. How do you make this decision?

Again, there is no infallible method – you simply have to work with what you know. That means constructing likely hands for declarer and your partner on the bidding, and trying to calculate where the tricks for the defence are going to come from.

When do you do this? If declarer is careful player, he will pause to plan his line of play at the first trick, usually before he plays from dummy. Make use of that time to plan your own defence. More generally, if at any time declarer or your partner stops to think, use that time for your own benefit also.

Sometimes, though, declarer plays rapidly in order to put you under pressure as fast as he can. You have no time to think, the bidding has been unrevealing, and suddenly you have to make a decision. There used to be a saying: 'When in doubt, play the ace.' This was almost certainly promulgated by declarers who wanted their opponents to do the wrong thing, for it is very poor advice. This is the rule to follow: If you don't know what to do – duck, and quickly.

Consider the first position shown above:

Dummy
♠ K J 3 2

You
♠ A 8 6 5

Declarer leads the ten towards dummy. It is right to play the ace only if declarer has a singleton and *if he has no other loser*. Even if he has a singleton and you play the ace, you have gained nothing if he can subsequently discard a loser on the king. On balance, it is far more likely that he has either a doubleton spade or a loser elsewhere, and your only chance then is to play low and hope that he will go wrong.

Post Mortem (continued)

Once Pat had ducked the ace of clubs, declarer was well on the way to defeat. He could, of course, have ensured ten tricks after ruffing the king of clubs – spade ruff with the ten, diamond to the queen, spade ruff with the king, club ruff with the ace, jack of hearts and so on. Perhaps he feared that the diamond lead was a singleton, not being aware of the weird 'reason' that had inspired Chris's choice. Perhaps he was playing for an overtrick, entirely reasonable at pairs scoring. The fact remained that by anticipating the problem in the club suit, Pat had earned the very good result that her side obtained.

The score

Plus 100 was a fine score for North–South. A couple of other declarers had managed to muddle the play to go down in four hearts, and one pair had gone down in five hearts trying for a slam. Chris wrote down eight out of ten in the estimates column, congratulated Pat on her defence, and sat back feeling quite pleased with life. East drank the rest of his beer.

'It's your round,' he said to West.

'There's another board yet,' said his partner.

'Details, always details,' sighed East.

Deal 10

Pat placed the tenth board on the table. She took her hand out of its slot, and arranged the cards thus:

Love All. Dealer East.

♠ A Q 6 5 3
♡ 7 5 2
♢ A J 8 7 5
♣ —

'One no-trump,' said East on Pat's left.

'Double,' said Chris firmly.

'Redouble,' said West.

'Just a minute,' thought Pat. 'How many points are there in this deck? Twelve to fourteen for East, sixteen or so for Chris, West must have about ten for that redouble and I've got eleven. That's fifty at least. Maybe I should call the Director and ask for a real pack of cards.'

'Did you hear my alert?' enquired East.

'Yes, of course,' said Pat, who hadn't. 'What does the redouble show, please?'

'It asks me to bid two clubs,' said East. 'He either has clubs, or diamonds and hearts, or both majors. He doesn't want to play in one no trump redoubled, though.'

'Pity,' thought Pat as she passed. No doubt they were in for a complicated auction, but she would wait to see what turned up.

'Two clubs,' said East.

'Double,' said Chris calmly.

Pat contemplated this development with some alarm. Should she pass this double, or try to show her suits? Perhaps a cue-bid of three clubs would be best, but that could get awkward . . .

'Two diamonds,' said West. East alerted again, and Pat heard it this time.

'Yes, please?' she enquired.

'In principle,' said East, 'diamonds and hearts. But if one of you doubles and he redoubles, then he has the major suits.'

'Well,' thought Pat, 'maybe he has. I know one thing, though – they are not going to make two diamonds.'

'Double,' she said, and there were two passes round to West who redoubled. East alerted, but since he had told everyone what that meant on the previous round, Pat did not need to ask any further questions. For the moment, she was quite happy to leave the opponents in two diamonds redoubled, so she passed.

East bid two hearts, and Chris now bid three clubs. West passed with the air of a man who had been unexpectedly reprieved from the gallows, and Pat considered a brand new problem. So far, the auction had been:

West	North	East	South
—	—	1 NT	Double
Redouble[1]	Pass	2♣[2]	Double
2◇[3]	Double	Pass	Pass
Redouble[4]	Pass	2♡	3♣
Pass	?		

[1] Clubs, or the red suits, or the majors
[2] Compulsory
[3] The red suits or the majors
[4] The majors

It had taken a while, but at least now everybody knew what was going on. East had a weak no-trump, Chris had a good hand with clubs, and West had a bad hand with the majors. What, though, was Pat to do now? Make up your mind before reading on.

Was there any point, wondered Pat, in bidding her spades? After all, West had shown the majors and East had at least two spades for his opening one no-trump, so Chris would not have spade support. Still, she had shown diamonds already by doubling two diamonds, so it could not hurt to do what came naturally by bidding her other suit.

'Three spades,' she said. East passed, and Chris bid three no-trumps. Would you take any further action on Pat's hand?

Eventually, Pat decided that she would bid on. After all, her double of two diamonds did not have to show a suit this long or this good, and there was no law against Chris having some diamond support.

'Four diamonds,' said Pat. Chris took a while over this, then emerged with four hearts. This had to be a cue-bid in the enemy heart suit – the only one that they had actually bid naturally – so Chris was showing some diamond support and some interest in a slam. What action would you now take?

Pat, as forthright a bidder as ever was, selected six diamonds from among alternatives. 'After all,' she told herself, 'the last time I jumped to a slam it made, and wouldn't it be fine if we could score two good results despite everything the opponents have done to make life difficult?'

East gave the bid of six diamonds a little thought, then shrugged his shoulders and passed. Everybody else passed also, East led the king of hearts, and Pat was confronted with another hand that looked far from straightforward:

♠ A Q 6 5 3
♡ 7 5 2
♢ A J 8 7 5
♣ —

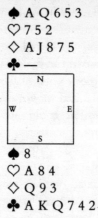

♠ 8
♡ A 8 4
♢ Q 9 3
♣ A K Q 7 4 2

West	North	East	South
—	—	1 NT	Double
Redouble[1]	Pass	2♣[2]	Double
2♢[3]	Double	Pass	Pass
Redouble[4]	Pass	2♡	3♣
Pass	3♠	Pass	3 NT
Pass	4♢	Pass	4♡
Pass	6♢	All Pass	

[1] Clubs, or the red suits, or the majors
[2] Compulsory
[3] The red suits or the majors
[4] The majors

How would you play this hand?

'It looks,' thought Pat, 'as though I have some work to do here. Still, at least I can be fairly sure where the high cards are. West has perhaps a jack or two and East has the rest. Moreover, West has long spades so it seems that East's king of spades must fall early. I think I will just take care of the heart losers first, then see what can be done if I cross-ruff a few tricks.'

Pat called for dummy's ace of hearts on the first trick, to

which West followed with the jack. She cashed dummy's ace
and king of clubs, throwing two hearts from her hand as both
opponents followed suit. It did not seem that it could hurt to
cash the queen of clubs also, so she did that and discarded a spade
as the opponents continued to follow. The ace of spades was
followed by a spade towards dummy, on which East's king
appeared for the full deal was:

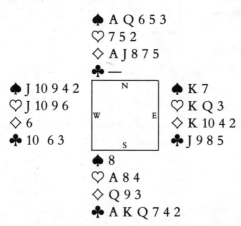

Pat ruffed a heart in her hand and continued with the queen of
spades, unable to resist a triumphant smile at Chris as she did so.
This was understandable, since the position now was:

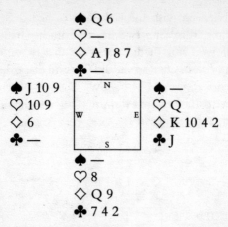

There was nothing East could do. If he ruffed low, declarer would overruff with nine, ruff a heart or a club back to hand and lead the last spade in this position:

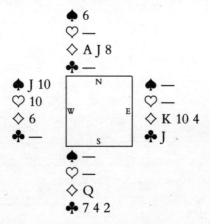

easily taking three of the last four tricks. If East ruffed with the king and exited with a trump, declarer would win in dummy with the nine, ruff a heart or a club low and cross-ruff the rest with high trumps. In practice, East threw a heart to leave:

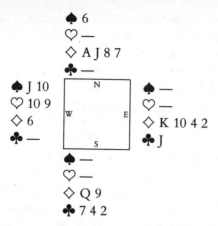

Pat ruffed her last spade in dummy with the nine, East throwing a club, and ran the queen of diamonds. East could win with the king, but had now to lead from ◇10 4 2 into declarer's ◇A J 8. Contract made.

'Well done again!' said Chris. 'You can play all the slams from now on.'

'Maybe some of them will be a bit easier,' said Pat, flushed with her success.

'Couldn't you just have bid two spades?' asked East grumpily of his partner. 'It's much more difficult for them to bid six diamonds then, and she wouldn't have known so much about the distribution.'

'I could have done,' retorted West, 'but you made me play this blasted system, and the last time I took out into my five-card suit you blamed me for not going through the rescue sequence. Anyway, two spades doubled costs a million.'

'They wouldn't have stood it doubled,' said East. 'He'd have bid three clubs and we would have been all right.'

Why was it, wondered Chris, that whenever a certain type of player obtained a bad result, the opponents ceased to exist? Or at any rate, were discussed as though they did not exist, with all kinds of assumptions made about what they would or would not do? Still, it could not be pleasant for the opponents to have recorded two dismal scores in a row, he reflected. Even the best of us might show a little exasperation under such circumstances.

Post Mortem

Many pairs these days, conscious of the fact that the weak no-trump can sometimes lead to a profitable penalty double for the opponents, have a conventional rescue mechanism to escape if one no-trump is doubled. Some of these rescues are very convoluted, involving all manner of bids in non-suits followed by rescue redoubles or bids in other non-suits.

Top class players have a number of devices to cope with this kind of thing, but what Pat and Chris did here has the merit of simplicity and effectiveness in most cases. If the opponents bid a suit that they might not have but you do, double them. In this way, you can take advantage of their contortions to show your own suits at a low level. When it appears that they have bid their real suit, stop and consider how best to proceed.

Try to avoid the fatal malaise known as 'doubling rhythm'. In auctions where you have gleefully doubled everything because you have A K Q 7 4 2, or A J 8 7 5, in the suit, always pause to consider whether it is worth doubling in a suit where you hold 7 5 2. Don't fall into the trap of thinking that you have them on the run – their manoeuvres are designed to locate their best fit, and if they find it then it may very well be worthwhile simply taking over and bidding you own hands.

Pat's decision to bid on over three no-trumps was courageous but probably correct. If Chris had a less suitable hand for diamonds, he would presumably have a stronger hand for play in no-trumps and could retreat to that denomination at the four level – certainly *not* Blackwood! By taking advantage of the information that the opponents' auction had given her, she was able to justify her forward bidding with some excellent play. Slightly lucky to find the nine of diamonds in dummy, though!

As to the behaviour of East and West after the hand, it was of course the height of bad manners. It is human nature to want to express dissatisfaction at a rotten result, and the impulse is generally to lash out at partner while ignoring the opponents. As usual, this is counter-productive – partner will not give of his best on the next deal, while the opponents will simply be determined to avenge the slight.

The score
Plus 920 was not quite a top for Pat and Chris, as it happened. At one table, West bid two diamonds immediately over one no-trump, then redoubled at his next turn to show the majors. Either East had not come across this manoeuvre before or he was having a quiet doze – whatever the reason, two diamonds redoubled became the final contract. The defence slipped a little and beat it only six tricks, but that was a penalty of 2800.

At another table, West was not blessed with any conventional rescue mechanism or any desire to experiment with an unconventional one. He simply rescued one no-trump doubled to two spades, and South did rather well to sit for North's penalty double of this contract. The defence was merciless, defeating the contract by five tricks and achieving an 1100 penalty.

So, Chris's estimate of ten on the board was a little optimistic. Still, his side was back on course after their awful start.

Deal 11

'Well, dear,' said East as she took her seat for the sixth round, 'and how are you getting on?'

'Oh, hello,' said Pat, recognizing the pair of elderly ladies who had moved into the East–West chairs. They had been playing at Pat and Chris's local club for as long as she could remember, and probably for as long as anyone could remember.

'Not so badly,' said Pat. 'A bit different from the club, though, isn't it?'

West, meanwhile, was engaging in the ritual which preceded every round of duplicate bridge that she played these days. Producing a bidding board and a coin from her capacious handbag, she addressed Chris:

'I'm afraid I'm a bit hard of hearing, so I hope you won't mind using these to bid with,' she said. Chris, used to this procedure and knowing the futility of a verbal reply, smiled and nodded his head.

A bidding board is a piece of hardboard marked with a rectangular grid, of which the horizontal rows are the bidding denominations – clubs, diamonds, hearts, spades and no-trumps – and the vertical columns are the numbers from one to seven. There are also spaces for Pass, Double, Redouble, Stop and Alert. You make a bid by placing the coin on the square that contains the call you wish to make. The device is a very useful one for players whose hearing is impaired.

Chris picked up his cards for the eleventh deal:

Game All. Dealer West.

♠ 8 7 3 2
♡ A 6
♢ 10 8 3
♣ A 7 6 5

West placed the coin on the bidding board in the square for an opening bid of 1♡. Pat moved it to the Pass square, and East in turn picked up the coin and moved it to the square for 2♣. The silence seemed eerie to Chris, amid the quiet murmur of verbal auctions being conducted in the rest of the room, but he had nothing to do but move the coin to the Pass square once again.

West moved the coin to 3♣, Pat passed and East bid 3♡. West bid 3 NT, but East returned the contract firmly to 4♡ with a decisive movement of the bidding coin.

What action would you take on Chris's hand at this point?

Chris picked up the bidding coin and was just about to drop it on the Pass square when a thought struck him. Opponents had bid and raised the club suit, so presumably would have eight cards there and Pat would have a singleton. If she led this card, Chris would be able to win the ace and give Pat a ruff. With the ace of hearts a sure trick, the defence would need only one more to defeat the contract, and perhaps this would come from a second club ruff, or Pat might have a high card somewhere.

With the air of a man producing a master bid, Chris doubled. It was something of a disappointment to have to do it silently – difficult to make an imposing penalty double when you had to do it by playing shove-ha'penny, thought Chris. Both West and East blinked a bit, but they were used to people doubling them and neither gave much thought to either a redouble or a conversion to 4 NT. The former would be an unheard-of risk, and the latter would be Blackwood.

Pat led the ♣2, a singleton sure enough, and East laid down an imposing dummy:

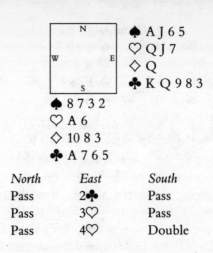

♠ A J 6 5
♡ Q J 7
◇ Q
♣ K Q 9 8 3

♠ 8 7 3 2
♡ A 6
◇ 10 8 3
♣ A 7 6 5

West	North	East	South
1♡	Pass	2♣	Pass
3♣	Pass	3♡	Pass
3 NT	Pass	4♡	Double
All Pass			

Chris won the club with the ace, declarer following with the
♣10, and considered his return. What card would you play in
his place?

'It looks,' thought Chris to himself, 'as though West has only
five hearts. With six, she would doubtless have bid 4♡ and not
3 NT over 3♡. That being so, if Pat ruffs the next club and
returns a heart to my ace, I can give her another ruff. But how
can I persuade her to do this?'

Chris selected the ♣6 for his return, and Pat ruffed as declarer
followed with the ♣J. Without seeming to give the position a
great deal of thought, Pat switched to a spade. This was the full
deal:

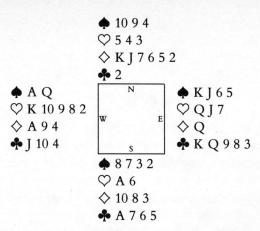

♠ 10 9 4
♡ 5 4 3
◇ K J 7 6 5 2
♣ 2

♠ A Q
♡ K 10 9 8 2
◇ A 9 4
♣ J 10 4

♠ K J 6 5
♡ Q J 7
◇ Q
♣ K Q 9 8 3

♠ 8 7 3 2
♡ A 6
◇ 10 8 3
♣ A 7 6 5

To Chris's horror, declarer played the ace and queen of spades, then the ace of diamonds. Crossing to the table with a diamond ruff, she discarded her remaining club on the ♠K and led a heart. There was nothing the defence could do now to defeat the contract and Chris, in unthinking rage at the ruin of his master plan, turned savagely on his partner.

'How could you play a spade?' he demanded. 'If I'd wanted a spade, I'd have returned a higher club than the six. I must have the ace of hearts to double this contract. All you had to do was play a trump, and we'd have got a top instead of this complete bottom. What's the use of my making these brilliant doubles if you're going to ruin them by not being able to find the simplest defences? Haven't you heard of suit preference signals – if I'd wanted a spade, I'd have played the seven of clubs back, not the six. I carefully chose the middle card to ask for the middle suit – hearts – but I might just as well have been playing with a brick wall.'

Pat bit her lip. She could, of course, have pointed out that declarer had played cleverly in following suit with the ♣J and ♣10 to the first two tricks. She had no way, in practice, of knowing what declarer's lowest club was, and therefore what

Chris's highest was. The club layout could have been:

♣ 2

♣ J 10 7   ♣ K Q 9 8 3

♣ A 6 5 4

in which case Chris's ♣6 would be the highest and would ask for a spade return. She knew from experience, though, that pointing this out would merely exasperate her partner further. Chris was normally able to keep his temper well in check, but once something had upset him, it was best to apologize and try to get on with things as fast as possible.

'Sorry, Chris,' she said. 'I should have worked it out. Let's play the next board, shall we?'

'How much is four hearts doubled?' asked West, who knew perfectly well how much it was, for despite her deafness and her scatterbrained air she was a very shrewd competitor. Seeing a promising argument between her opponents apparently about to be avoided, she felt that a little stirring of the pot might not come amiss. But Chris was back in control of himself, and already beginning to feel guilty about his outburst. He showed the scoresheet to West with the figures '790' entered in the East–West column, smiled benevolently at her, and put the board away.

Post Mortem

The East–West auction was normal enough. West had an awkward choice over her partner's 2♣ response – not quite strong enough for 2 NT, it seemed to her better to show the club support than to rebid a relatively poor heart suit.

This kind of bid is frequently overlooked by Acol players who use a weak no-trump with four card majors, but it is often the simplest and most effective way to progress the auction. You will not miss a 5–3 heart fit, since partner can always continue with heart support as in this case, and if a heart fit does not exist then the knowledge that you have some club support may enable partner to bid 3 NT with confidence.

East could not bid 4♡ immediately over her partner's 3♣, since this would promise four-card support, an example of the treatment known as the Delayed Game Raise. 3♡ was forcing, though, so East was able to place the contract in 4♡ eventually.

Sequences for discussion

You and your partner should agree on the meaning of sequences which follow the patterns:

West	East		West	East
1X	1Y	or	1X	2Y
2Y	3X		3Y	3X

since even the experts are not all agreed on these sequences. For example:

West	East
1♡	2♣
3♣	3♡

is played by some as non-forcing, and it would be galling to find that while you play it as forcing, your partner does not.

If you decide that such a sequence should be forcing, then you will need to discuss the implications of this auction:

West	East
1♡	2♣
3♣	4♡

Since 3♡ would be forcing, a jump to 4♡ can convey a specific meaning. A common treatment is that it is a Delayed Game Raise, mentioned above and usually abbreviated to DGR. The name derives from the fact that you delay raising 1♡ immediately to 4♡ because you have a club suit that you consider worthy of mention since it may be the key to a possible slam. For example:

♠ 3 2
♡ A J 6 5
♢ 5 4
♣ A K J 4 3

would be an ideal hand for this DGR sequence.

If you decide to play Delayed Game Raises, there are other sequences of which you need to be aware. For example:

West	East
1♡	2♣
2♡	4♡

is *not* a DGR because 3♡ woiuld not be forcing, whereas:

West	East
1♡	2♣
2 NT	4♡

can be a DGR if you play them because 3♡ would be forcing.

Post Mortem (continued)

Chris's double was a sound gamble, especially at pairs scoring, since it stood a good chance of outscoring those pairs who had been less oppotunistic or had less revealing bidding. The opponents did not *have* to have eight clubs, but the odds were high that they did. Even if the defence's second club ruff failed to materialise, there was no reason why Pat might not produce a defensive trick. Unfortunately, neither of these chances materialised. There was nothing Pat could do about not having a side trick – she had simply not been dealt one. Might she have found the defence that her partner so desperately wanted her to find – a trump return at the third trick?

Suit preference signals

This subject has been covered perhaps more extensively than any other in the literature of the game, and I am certainly not going to rehash it here. Let us just remind ourselves of the basic principle: If, either by your discard or by the card you play when leading or following suit, you wish to convey to partner information about your side suit strength – your *preference* for the suit partner should attack next – then you play a high card to show interest in a higher-ranking suit, a low card to show interest in a lower-ranking suit.

This is fine as far as it goes, and that is as far as most players take it. There are many possible extensions to the idea, and it is worth looking at some of them.

First, the problem that faced Chris on this hand. Normally, when you are a defender and you win partner's singleton club lead with hearts as trumps, then your choice is between returning a high club to ask for a spade back, and a low club to ask for a diamond. But suppose you don't want a spade or a diamond – you actually want a trump?

This is very difficult, for somehow defenders do not think of returning a *trump* to put partner in for a ruff. After all, if partner can win the first trump then they will still get their ruff, won't they?

Most of the time, yes. But if declarer can discard in the suit where the ruff is threatened, then the ruff may disappear, as happened on this deal. So, if you are a defender and you want to put partner in for a second ruff, do not dismiss the possibility that his entry may be in trumps and that it may be necessary to find it now.

Can we signal for a trump return, though? Well, Chris did his best. He had a choice of the seven, the six and the five of clubs to return at trick two, and it seemed reasonable to think: 'The seven – the highest card – would ask for a spade; the five – the lowest card – would ask for a diamond; so the six – the middle card – should ask for a heart, the middle suit.' Do you disagree with this reasoning?

You shouldn't, for it is sound enough and an important principle to bear in mind. Often – more often than you probably believe – there are *three* suits among which you want to express a preference, not merely two, and if you have enough possible cards to signal for one of three suits then you can and should do so. Moreover, situations arise in which you don't actually want *any* suit attacked by partner – your hand is bereft of values and you simply want partner to follow his own devices. You can try to tell him this by giving a suit preference signal for a suit that you can't possibly want attacked, and hope that he gets the message – you can't want this, therefore you don't want anything.

Expert players use suit preference signals in a great variety of positions, some of which you might like to think about for yourselves. For example, if declarer is just about to run dummy's solid suit, don't wait until your first discard to give suit preference – do it by the order in which you follow to dummy's cards. By the time you make *your* first discard, your partner may already have had to make two or three, and he may very well make the wrong ones unless you give him some help. Here is a simple example – take the East seat:

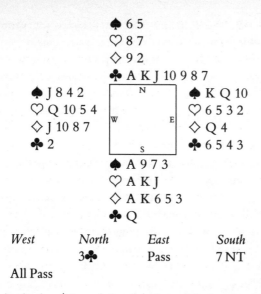

```
              ♠ 6 5
              ♡ 8 7
              ◇ 9 2
              ♣ A K J 10 9 8 7
♠ J 8 4 2          N          ♠ K Q 10
♡ Q 10 5 4                    ♡ 6 5 3 2
◇ J 10 8 7   W         E      ◇ Q 4
♣ 2                S         ♣ 6 5 4 3
              ♠ A 9 7 3
              ♡ A K J
              ◇ A K 6 5 3
              ♣ Q
```

West	North	East	South
	3♣	Pass	7 NT
All Pass			

West leads the ◇J, and South wins with the ace. He leads the ♣Q to dummy's ace and is clearly about to run the rest of the suit. If West is playing with a partner who will give him no help, then he will have an impossible discard as early as the third round of clubs (he can spare a heart on the second, but anything could be fatal on the third). That is why, as East, you should play your clubs in the order 6, 5, 4, 3 – not to show that you have four, since everyone will know this by the end of trick three anyway, but to show by playing your highest club at every turn that you can guard the highest-ranking suit, spades. Now West can throw his spades away happily, and will later be discarding after South in the red suits, so there can be no squeeze and the contract will fail.

You can do this sort of this when declarer is drawing trumps – I expect that many of you play that a peter in trumps shows an odd number, or asks for a ruff. But what do you do when you obviously aren't going to get a ruff and when it is clear that by the time trumps have been drawn your partner will know that you had an odd number in any case? Try playing your trumps in suit-preference fashion to indicate where your outside strength lies, and see how much less often your partner struggles with his discards or returns the wrong thing when he gets in.

Post Mortem (continued)

Of course, declarer must not sit idly by and watch as the defenders signal to each other with the precision that I have described above. You must always be on the watch for ways to jam the enemy communications, and one of the simplest requires almost no effort at all compared with the effect it produces. Defenders can only draw inferences from their partner's selected card if they know what the selection was made from, and you can keep this knowledge from them by the simplest expedient of *not invariably following suit with your lowest card*. That is all, and yet the difference it makes is considerable.

On this deal, for example, if declarer had followed to the clubs 'upwards', with the four and the ten, Pat would have known that Chris's six was his middle card and might have drawn the right conclusion. But declarer concealed the four for two rounds and Pat could not tell with certainty what was happening. If you keep the advice above in mind next time you play, you may find that those experts who always did the right thing against you in the past are finding it a little harder now.

Of Chris's emotional outburst, we will be charitable and say little. One of the most galling experiences in bridge is to take a daring risk which would have been a triumphant success had not partner obtusely turned it into a crushing disaster, and at such times it is difficult for even the most saintly among us to remember that what was obvious from one side of the table may not have been at all clear from the other, and that partner is still on our side.

The score

Chris was already ashamed of himself as he writes down a round zero in his estimates column. Alas, this proved an exactly accurate assessment, for at the only other table where four hearts were doubled by an opportunistic South, the contract was defeated. It was not that North found the heart return after ruffing the second club – it was just that declarer forgot to discard his remaining club on a spade before playing a trump!

Deal 12

Pat was hoping for an innocuous deal to give both herself and her partner time to calm down after the tension of the previous board. The cards that she picked up, however, indicated that once again her side would have to make the decisions:

♠ K Q 10
♡ A K 4 3
♢ A J 10 2
♣ 7 5

The question of which of two touching suits to open on a balanced hand is one that has occupied expert minds for many years, and the debate has generated far more heat than light. Pat was blissfully unaware of this, though. She and Chris played four-card majors so that they could open with a major when they were dealt one, and Pat did not intend to break the habits of a lifetime now.

'One heart,' she said. East passed and Chris responded two clubs. West passed and Pat felt that she had a slight problem. What action would you take on her hand?

Of course, the hand was a balanced 17 count, and such a point count indicates a rebid of 2 NT. There were good reasons, however, for regarding the hand as worth more than its face value – the A J 10 of diamonds was a combination that could easily be worth two tricks and the K Q 10 of spades was a good holding. Moreover, a hand with its points all working together – touching honour combinations, honours in long suits – usually has a higher value than the point count would suggest. For these reasons, Pat felt inclined to stretch a point and rebid 3 NT.

This was perfectly sensible thinking, for Pat had a good understanding of hand evaluation and was, as we have seen, not backward in coming forwards where bidding was concerned. However, she suppressed her natural instincts and rebid 2 NT for a reason that had little to do with bridge itself.

'I'd normally bid 3 NT,' she thought, 'but I'd better not. If it doesn't work out well, when Chris finds out I only had seventeen points he'll go completely bonkers after that last board. Better to stick by the rules this time, and hope nothing goes wrong.'

So Pat rebid 2 NT, which her partner raised to 3 NT without pause for cogitation. East, though, seemed to give her opening lead considerable thought before emerging with the two of spades. Chris put down dummy, and Pat saw with amusement that her rebid had not mattered at all, for the final contract would have been the same in any case:

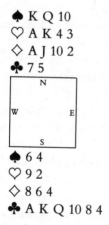

♠ K Q 10
♡ A K 4 3
◇ A J 10 2
♣ 7 5

♠ 6 4
♡ 9 2
◇ 8 6 4
♣ A K Q 10 8 4

West played the nine on East's spade lead, and Pat won the trick with the ten. She led the ♣7 and East followed with the ♣6. How would you play 3 NT in Pat's place?

This is actually a difficult problem, but only because of the method of scoring. Since after the lead Pat had two certain spade tricks, two hearts and a diamond, it was clear that four club tricks would be enough to bring the total to nine and a completely safe play exists, once East has followed, to ensure four tricks. Simply finesse the ten – if West wins, even with a singleton jack, the rest of the suit will run. If the ten holds and West follows, there are six tricks – and if the ten holds and West shows out, you still have four tricks.

Incidentally, there is also a completely safe play for *five* tricks in the suit once East follows to the first round. Can you work this out for yourself? The answer will appear later.

But safe plays – or *safety plays* as they are called at bridge – are often quite the opposite at pairs. Playing for money, you should of course do all in your power to ensure that you make the game or slam contract you have reached. If this means giving up a trick you need not have lost on a friendly lie of cards to guard against an unfriendly one, then you should do just that. Playing for match points, though, you cannot afford to make plays that will give up tricks more often than not – for more often than not, this means that you will score fewer tricks than the declarers with your cards who play for normal distributions. Taking a safety play to ensure plus 600 in 3 NT will score you a zero if the field, taking the less safe line, scores 630 or 660.

Back at the table, Pat was thinking. 'That spade lead,' she mused, 'seemed to take a while. Not only that, it looks as though it was from ♠ A J 9 8 – a very dangerous holding. I wonder if East was reluctant to lead a heart instead because I opened the bidding in that suit?

'At any rate, it looks as though the lead has given me a trick that declarers at other tables might not be given. Therefore, it may not matter so much if I give up a club trick – that's only giving back the trick I was given on the lead, after all. And if clubs do break badly, we should score a nice top! So, although I wouldn't normally do it, I'll finesse the ♣10. First of all I didn't bid 3 NT, now I take a safety play – I hope that Chris is watching all this and seeing that I can be discplined if I have to be.'

Do you agree with Pat's reasoning? Make up your mind before you see the full deal, for you will surely agree with the result to which it led:

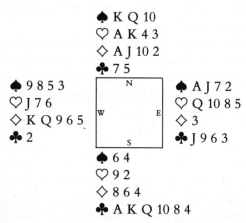

```
              ♠ K Q 10
              ♡ A K 4 3
              ◇ A J 10 2
              ♣ 7 5
  ♠ 9 8 5 3        N        ♠ A J 7 2
  ♡ J 7 6                   ♡ Q 10 8 5
  ◇ K Q 9 6 5   W     E     ◇ 3
  ♣ 2              S        ♣ J 9 6 3
              ♠ 6 4
              ♡ 9 2
              ◇ 8 6 4
              ♣ A K Q 10 8 4
```

When the ♣10 held and West showed out on the next club, Pat could hardly suppress a cry of elation. She had eleven tricks available now, and she made no mistake in taking them.

'Well done, dear!' said East. 'A safety play, was it?'

'Yes, actually, it was,' said Pat a little self-importantly. 'I had to think about the lead, you see, and it seemed to me . . .'

She broke off, for her partner appeared to be trying hard not to choke to death. 'Are you all right, Chris?' she enquired. 'I know it's not often I do the right thing, but every once in a while it happens, you know.'

'Absolutely,' said Chris, who had regained his self-control. 'Well done indeed, partner – beautifully played.'

He took out the score sheet and entered plus 660 in a North–South column otherwise devoid of plus scores. Folding it up again, he immediately engaged East in a long conversation on the subject of gardening, which he knew was East's abiding passion although he himself was to horticulture what Albert Einstein was to water polo. With her partner and her right hand opponent engrossed in the problems of aphid control, Pat found herself frustrated in her desire to explain how clever she had been. She turned to West.

'You see,' she said, 'I took the safety play because I thought the lead had given me . . .'

West, oblivious, picked up her bidding board and put it in her handbag. She smiled and nodded goodbye to Pat, then wandered off apparently aimlessly – but in reality to be first in the queue for the tea and biscuits which were served at the half-time interval. Pat gave it up.

Post Mortem

The subject of safety plays at pairs scoring is a difficult one, as we have said, though a good rule of thumb is simply to avoid them. Let us look at the mathematics of a deal similar to the one above, but simpler:

South is in 3 NT and a spade is led. West follows when South leads the ♣7 from hand. How should South play?

Since South requires five club tricks for the contract, at any form of scoring other than pairs he can follow the completely safe line for five tricks that you were asked to work out earlier – that is, to duck the first trick. If East wins with anything, the rest of the suit will run, and if East shows out on the first round then South can finesse the ten when next in.

At pairs, though, your object is *not*, first and foremost, to make your contract. Your object is to score better than the pairs sitting your way and holding your cards. You should reason along these lines: Am I in the 'normal' contract – the one that all or most of the pairs holding our cards will reach? If so, then I should play to give myself the best chance of scoring the maximum number of matchpoints. If not, then I must consider what the normal contract is and how I can outscore the pairs playing in it.

We will return to the second part of that process later. For the moment, we will look at the play of a normal contract, which 3 NT certainly is, both on Pat's hand and our example.

The phrase above, 'the best chance of scoring the maximum number of matchpoints', may sound straightforward, but it is not. Suppose that a deal arises on which there is a line – call it line A – that gives a 40 per cent chance of nine tricks. If it fails, however, you will make only seven tricks. An alternative line B is 100 per cent guaranteed to make exactly eight tricks, no more and no fewer. Which line should you follow?

Playing to go down

Mathematicians use the term 'expectation' to denote the average outcome if the same event happens a number of times and the results go exactly according to the laws of probability. Thus, if you bet £100 on your lucky number at roulette, your 'expectation' is a return of £97.30 even though you will obviously not be given this sum. You will be given £3,600 if your number comes up and nothing if it does not. If, though, you played for thirty-seven spins and each number including yours came up once, then it would cost you £3,700 to win that £3,600. You are thus losing money at the rate of £100 per thirty-seven spins, or $\frac{1}{37}$ of £100 per spin – so your 'expectation' for any single spin is a return of $\frac{36}{37}$ of your stake.

Your expectation for following line A cannot be calculated precisely, for it depends on the number of other pairs who follow line A as opposed to line B. Suppose first that there are six tables in the field, so a top on a board is ten. If you are the only player to follow line A, then you will score a top 40 per cent of the time and a bottom the other 60 per cent. In 100 deals, this will give you a total of 400 match points and your expectation is therefore four match points per deal. All the other pairs will score six match points 60 per cent of the time – 360 match points over 100 deals – and four match points 40 per cent of the time – 160 match points over 100 deals. Their expectation is thus $\frac{520}{100} = 5.2$ match points per deal.

Now suppose that only one player follows line B. You and all the other line A players will score six match points 40 per cent of the time – 240 match points over 100 deals – four match points 60 per cent of the time – another 240 match points. Your expectation is now 480 match points over the 100 deals, or 4.8 match points per deal. The solitary follower of line B scores a top 60 per cent of the time – 600 match points – and a bottom the other 40 per cent of the time, so his expectation is now $\frac{600}{100} =$ six match points per deal.

Finally, suppose that half of you follow line A and half line B. You will score eight match points 40 per cent of the time – 320 over 100 deals – and two match points 60 per cent of the time for a total of 440 match points over 100 deals and an expectation of 4.4 per deal. The line B merchants will score two match points 40 per cent of the time – 80 match points over 100 deals – and eight match points 60 per cent of the time for a total of 560 match points and an expectation of 5.6 per deal.

It should have struck you by now that however many of you follow line A, you *never* expect to score more than the followers of line B. You may outscore them on one *particular* deal, but in the long run you will inevitably lose to them. Moreover, although the number of match points you score varies according to the number of line A players, the *difference* between your expectation and that of the line B adherents is always the same. Line A is 1.2 match points per deal worse than line B.

I make no apology for setting out the mathematics in detail. It is important that you try to follow the argument, for its conclusion may startle you and it is not something that you should simply take on trust, since you will find this very difficult if not impossible:

If you judge that you are in the 'normal' 3 NT – two balanced hands each of thirteen points, say – and you can see that your only chance for the contract is less than 50 per cent and will lead to an extra one down if it fails, then you should *deliberately play for one down!* This may seem repellent to your notion of what the game of bridge is about, but the logic is inescapable. It may very well happen that the best line of play at pairs in a normal contract is *not* the line that gives you the best – or only – chance of making the contract. Consider this deal:

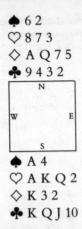

♠ 6 2
♡ 8 7 3
♢ A Q 7 5
♣ 9 4 3 2

♠ A 4
♡ A K Q 2
♢ K 3 2
♣ K Q J 10

South opens 2 NT and North raises to 3 NT – normal enough bidding, and you can be sure that the auction will be the same at just about every table. Unfortunately, the ♠5 is led and you can see that there is just one chance for the contract: the hearts and the diamonds must divide 3–3. Playing for money, your line of play would be clear. Win the second spade and cash the red suits. If they both break, take your nine tricks. If not, then you will have set up an extra trick for the opponents when you knock out the ♣A, and you will go an extra one down, but an investment of 100 points to gain a vulnerable game is clearly worth while.

Playing pairs, your line of play is equally clear. Win the second spade and knock out the ♣A, going one down gracefully. You could, of course, cash two rounds of both hearts and diamonds, but even if both opponents follow all the way, the chances of a 3–3 break in either suit remain less than 50 per cent (42.3 per cent to be precise), and the risk involved in cashing the third round of either is simply not worth it. You will make a trick fewer than the field more often than you will make a trick more, and as we saw above this means that you will score fewer match points than they do in the long run.

Post Mortem (continued)

Now, was Pat's play in 3 NT right or wrong? Obviously it was very right on the actual hand, so we will leave her to enjoy her triumph – which was exactly what Chris was doing when he had his choking fit. He had seen what his partner had not, that although the spade lead had given her a trick and made it possible to ensure her contract, the finesse of the ♣10 was nevertheless an error. It would gain a trick – in fact, it would gain two or three tricks – when either East or West had ♣J x x x, but it would lose a trick when West had ♣J, ♣J x or ♣J x x. The 4–1 break is about a 22.6 per cent chance, while the chance of West holding the unguarded jack is about 36.5 per cent, so Pat had followed a line which would result in taking fewer tricks than the field more often than not. As I hope you are by now convinced, this is losing strategy in the long run.

As I am sure you are convinced, the mathematics of match point tactics is a very complex subject. There are excellent books available which you can study should you wish to increase your knowledge. For the moment, we will leave Pat and Chris to enjoy their tea break. After his performance on board eleven, Chris very wisely decided against pointing out to Pat that her brilliancy was in fact a misplay. One thing was certain – his estimate of ten for this board was every bit as accurate as his zero for the previous one, and our pair are by no means out of the hunt. But to find out how the second half of the event turned out for them, I am afraid you will have to wait for the next book!